True

MW00988311

Inheritance

Dr. Charles S. Hanson

Contents

CHAPTER 1:

A FORTUNE

TO BE

INHERITED

The dream began peacefully. The meadow he and

his wife were walking in was knee deep in super-bloom.
Lupine and poppies licked at their knees leaving a coating
of golden pollen across shins and pooling on sneakers.
Humming birds xoated ne,t to them wondering what
these strangey xightless creatures were doing trudging
across their food supplA. z hawk swooped in the distance

then e,ploded in a frenPA of brown and red feathers
before theA heard the shotgun blast.

jhilip Wolted so hard that the hammock he was sleeping
in tipped and spun. The meadowy his wife Heathery and

the e,ploded bird disappeared when his chin planted
in the decomposed granite under him. 'hA hadn?t he
planted rAe grassy a much softer cushion for life?s sudden
fallsE

zs he stoody the realities of a head full of worries

marched through his mind. 'as his uncle Slon reallA
deadE He seemed so livelA a week ago when theA had
talked on the phone. 9prA was the word. Slon had alwaAs
been sprAy even at 2N. Rowy onlA seven daAs latery he was
in his grave. Rot ashes to ashesy but embalmedy faciallA
perfected with Devlony and laid to rest. "id he know he
was going to dieE jrobablA not. He seemed perfectlA
healthA. He had never even talked about death or last
wishes. z Aear ago he had told jhilip that he wanted his
"holdingsO to be split between jhilip and his two sisters.
He also wanted his two e,-wives to have a portion of his
estate. 1ther than thaty jhilip had assumed that Slon
would live to be 0YY.

'ith these thoughts and more plaAing ping pong in his

mindy jhilip stretchedy dusted oC his Weansy and headed
for the kitchen. zs he opened the screen doory he was
greeted bA fortA pounds of bark coming from the familA?s
eight pound 7orkie who seemed to be fullA recuperated

9

todaA. jhilip took a minute to rexect on his dog?s recent troubles. Three nights ago the dogy Mhewiey had raided the pantrA. The door should never have been left open. The pooch found a sealed four pound bag of dark chocolate chipsy tore it openy and ate about a pound. 9hortlA afterwardy he barfed prettA much all over the kitchen and dining room and passed out near the front door.

zfter thaty "eclany the couple?s 0I Aear old high school
Wuniory came home from basketball practicey opened the
doory tripped over poor Mhewiey and managed to land
one foot in the middle of a puddle of emulsiUed chocolate
puke. He picked up the lifeless pup and Aelledy " Vomy
dady there?s something wrong with Mhewie.O The dog
opened one eAey closed ity then vomited down the front
of "eclan?s WerseA. $n minutes all were in the 9:B headed
to the veterinarA S.D. The ne,t daA and 8NYYY latery
Mhewie was homey still needing anti-nausea medicines
and anti-convulsives. znd jhilip was seriouslA thinking
about leaving the side gate to the backAard open.

jhilip realiPed that he was daAdreaming. He reached

down and petted Mhewie as he entered the kitchen. He
thoughty "Thank goodness for :ncle Slon?s will. 'e?ll
make it through another vet bill.O Then he realiPed what
he was thinking. He should not at all be thankful that
Slon died. He had enough moneA from his law practice.
TheA were a thriving familA. His wife?s earnings as MountA
Moroner matched his.

jhilip parked himself at the kitchen tabley fed Mhewie

his anti-nausea pill wrapped in spreadable 9wiss cheesey
picked up the local newspaper and began to read. The

headlines were boldy double blacky and triple height.

TheA read5

ELON MCMURPHY DEAD AT 92. HUMBLE, QUIET

MAN LEAVES BEHIND HUGE UNEXPECTED FORTUNE.

jhilip pulled the paper closer seeking details. His

uncle had never indicated riches or possessions. 'hat
fortuneE How had he come bA the accumulated wealthE
'as this a hoa,E 9urelA this newspaper reporter was
talking about someone else. VaAbe this was an internet
glitch5 a wrong entrA herey a bad keA punch therey or
a website downloaded bA mistake. He xipped to page
three to Und the storA continued in magnifAing glass print
in 9ection q. The font looked to be siPe K or lower.
He guessed that the newspaper editor wanted the ads
that Ulled the page in large print more than more details
about an old man who died. $nterestinglAy the large print
ads proclaimedy

"qecome a millionaire in 4 Aears with these 4 easA
steps.O

Ten minutes of magniUed reading revealed that Slon?s

fortune might be real. The writer fullA identiUed Slon.
His address came Ursty then his age and birthdate. His
mother?s name and maiden name were ne,ty then the car
he drove. Sven the name of his dog appeared. 1nce Slon
was solidlA over-identiUedy the writer 3uoted a mAsteri-
ous source who said that he knew how "Vr. VcVurphA

13

had accumulated his holdings which are probablA e3ual
to the wealth in (ing 9olomon?s mines.O

jhilip shook his head at the e,aggerationy but he kept

on reading. "Vr. VcVurphA admired 'arren quCett for
the past)Y Aears. He Ugured that anAone who would sell
golf balls and deliver newspapers as a kid to get a start

had to be 1.(. He liked the things that Vr. quCett did5
0. Ro nouveau riche displaA of wealth. N. 9ame car and
house for most of his life. G. Ro spoiling of his kids Funtil
late in life!.). $nvestments in 9ee?s MandA and Moca Mola.
4. The fact that Vr. quCett might as well be called Vr.
—eico or 9ir zmerican S,press. Slon VcVurphA dreamed
of being 'arren quCett. q:T there was an enormous
diCerence. Slon was a true introvert. He was shA and
would do anAthing to avoid limelight. He decided to be
a 3uiety backseat quCett. 'or)Y Aears he purchased
qerkshire HathawaA shares through a private investor
with the agreement that no one should know about the
arrangement. zs of this date Vr. VcVurphA?s estate
holds)YYY shares of prime qerkshire HathawaA stoc
k.Ojhilip dropped the newspaper on the tabley rubbed
his temples with both Ustsy and grabbed his iVac. 9low
internet connection made him wait an eternal three minutes. He opened the search engine and in seconds found
out that a single share of qerkshire HathawaA was selling
for 80yNI0y0KN.)K. That meant that)YYY shares would
total nearlA Uve billion dollars. jhilip grabbed his i-phone
and pressed the speed dial for his wife. He had to leave
a message on her hairstAlist?s answering service.

zt that moment the basement door xew open and out

bounded jhilip?s 0I Aear old who Aelledy ""ady Aou are
not going to believe thisJ There?s a rumor on 'acebook
that :ncle Slon was rich. Rot Wust a little bit. Think Slon
Vusk. Think of owning mansions and a 'errari. jiPPa
seven nights a week. Deal moneAJO

"7esy maAbe so. qut what happened to all of those

values we have been teaching Aou*like help Aour neigh-
borsy give to the poory be humble in life and rich in spirit.O

"7ehy Aehy AehyO smarted "eclan with his head shaking

in circles. " ust look at it this waAy dad. 'e?ll have enough
moneA to un-poor the poor and drive a Lambo.O

The phone rang. jhilip gave a time out signal us-

ing both hands. "$t?s Aour mother calling me back.O He
grabbed his celly pressed the connect icony and saidy
"9weethearty we reallA need to talk.O

The deep baritone on the other end of the line intonedy

"9iry this is MlaAton q. 'eatherbourney attorneA for the
estate of Slon VcVurphA. zm $ speaking to jhilip VcVur-
phAEO

"1hy sorrAy $ was e,pecting a call from mA wife. 7esy this
is jhilipy jhilip VcVurphA.O

"—oody but mA call is for both Aou and Aour wife.O
"'elly siry she is having her hair done. How maA $ help
AouEO

'eatherbourne cleared his throaty coughing a bit too
loudlA into the phone. "$ must meet with both of Aou.O

17

"9he will be home soon. $ will check with her. $ know tomorrow is open.O

"Vr. VcVurphAy this is urgent. Man we possiblA meet

todaA at three. $t is about Aour uncle?s last will and testament. qecause there is alreadA a bit of furor about the amount of wealth Aour uncle has amassedy $ need to meet with Aou and all concerned parties. Row. TodaA. 'e need to head oC the media storm that is headed our waA.O

TRUE INHERITANCE 7

jhilip whistled in a deep breath. "1.(. 'e will be there.

'ill Aou please te,t me the location.O

The line went dead. jhilip rang back and received a

recording.

CHAPTER 2:

THANK GOD

FOR

i-PHONES

Philip jumped wh en his phone chi med again, not

because it was particularly loud, but because he was

sitting on it again. The damned thing had a mind of its own. When it should be on the table, it was under his butt buzzing. When he was downstairs, it was always upstairs. When he was in the garage, the phone found its way into the kitchen. Impossible. A leash would help.

He grabbed under his fanny, out came the phone, and he saw that it was Heather returning his call.

"You rang?" shouted Heather too close to her phone. Philip could hear people laughing loudly in the back-ground on her end of the call.

"Hi babe, sounds like a party.'

"No dear, what Melanie just said is hilarious. Look up
the work "merkin." You'll laugh. So what's up?"

"Did you receive a call or text from a lawyer named
Weatherbourne?"

"No such call," Heather chuckled trying to hold back
tears.

"He just called me because Uncle Elon died."
Heather responded with rote empathy, "He was 92. He
lived a long, full life. I hope he didn't suBer."

"No way to tell. All I know is that he was here one day,

gone the next. Out that is only part of why I am calling.
His lawyer wants to explain Elon's will today at three."

"Ch honey, can't it wait. I've got a pickleball tour-

nament with Oetty and Suzanne at three. Oesides, we
already know that we'll inherit that banged up old pickup
and grandma's chipped !hina. We might get something
from the sale of his house."

"WhoaR Hold on. This lawyer says that it will be much

more than that. I'll explain when you are here. Keally,
we don't have a choice. I think everyone else is going to
meet with Weatherbourne at three."

"C.3. C.3. I'll come home as soon as I can," said

Heather. She twirled her cell phone into her purse and told the empty passenger seat of her OMW MZ, "Nothing could be that important." She drove straight to Starbucks for a triple cream Latte with a pinch of cinnamon.

Philip was about to make his second call when Declan

dragged in his nine year old brother, 3eegan, by his shirt collar.

"What has he done now?" demanded Philip.

"He was bragging to his friends that within a year he

will own a Lamborghini and be practicing burning rubber on his dad's private race track."

"That's a little crazy, 3eegan," said dad tapping the side of his head with his index Jnger.

"NCT !KAGY, dad. 1ust look at the internet," said 3ee-gan doing a great Oill :ates imitation.

Philip stopped. He knew that his boy had found out

about Elon's fortune. He said, "Let's not go nuts. We don't even know if this inheritance is real or not. We meet with the lawyer at Z today. Would you like to go with us?"

3eegan levitated. His Nike Airs were bouncing up about six inches oB the ground.

"Heck yes, yes, yes," shouted 3eegan. "Should I go wait in the car?"

Declan, who was always full of mischief said, "Sure, you go right ahead." Three o'clock was a long way oB.

Philip looked at his watch. It was already 0qZF. He

knew he had to make contact with his sisters and Elon's ex-wives within the next hour. He decided that family should come Jrst. Out which sister? 3aran could keep

24

the :oodyear blimp suspended in midair with her loud
persistent stream of conversation. Marielle would be
busy with her three young children, a boy, a girl, and
one she referred to as Satan. A call to her might be
Jve minutes or it could take ZF minutes on hold while
Marielle tried to secure Satan with duct tape and rope,
her terms for ade—uate child restraint. She talked about
her youngest as a boy with the energy of a Tasmanian
Devil. She referred to him as "Wombat" and "4erret."

Philip decided 3aran should come Jrst. She was oldest

and might be oBended if her younger sister found out

what was happening before she did.

He called herXready for a one sided conversation.

This sibling could say more words in one minute than a

weather station announcer just before a tornado. The

machine gun voice started with

" H e l -

lo-its-been-nine-days-and-Jve-hours-since-you-last-

c a l l e d - m e - I - c o u l d - h a v e - V o w n - t o - ! a m b o -

dia-and-back-in-that-much-time-you-need-to-treat-

your-siblings-with-more-respect." All Z words were

pronounced at one big, long multi-syllable

conglomerate. No pauses. No punctuation. It was like

facing gunJre at the shooting range.

To compensate, Philip said one word, "DIDYCUHEAK-

4KCMELCN'SLAWYEK."

" Y E S - I - H E A K D - W E - A K E - K I ! H - I ' L L - K E -

P L A ! E - T H E - T I K E S - C N - M Y - 4 C K D - 4 C -

! U S - A N D - P A Y - C 4 4 - S C M E - C 4 - M Y - ! K E D -

IT-!AKDS-I'LL-OE-THEKE-AT-THKEE." She hung up.

Philip thumped his phone side ear with his palm trying

to knock the jangle out of his brain. He decided to text

Marielle, his sweet sisterq

HI SWEET SISTER. I TRUST THAT YOU HEARD FROM

**UNCLE ELON'S LAWYER. WE ARE ALL TO MEET HI
M AT**

**HIS LAW OFFICE, 3301 MAIN STREET, AT 3 TODAY. S
AD**

NEWS BUT EXCITING. SEE YOU THERE.

In minutes she texted back, **"NANNY WILL CAGE SA-TAN. DO YOU HAVE ANY RITALIN?"**

Philip laughed aloud. His sister had a wicked sense of humor.

Now came the hard partq THE E -WI ES Jamboree Jane

1ones and Sarah !.. He knew what was coming. Ooth were bitter. Ooth were argumentative. Imagining which one would be more pleasant to talk to was not in the chips, so he made an alphabetical decision. 1.1. would be Jrst.

"Hello 1am, it's been a while," Philip started with buttery smoothness. It did not work.

Her megaphone loud reply was, "NCW SCN, you know

that half of that estate is mineR I took care of that old man for two and a half whole years while he recuperated. He owes me for that."

Philip was not sure how to reply. 4irst, he was not her

son. His birth mother had passed away ten years back. Second, Elon was never sick. There was no recuperating. Third, 1amboree and Elon were married for only one and a half yearsR He swallowed hard and said, "I hear you, but let's wait until the Jnal will is shared. 4or all I know you may be right." Then he took a chance and cautiously continued, "Out there is a possibility that you are wrong." The explosion happened. "That's crazy. If you think

that you can manipulate what is owed to me, you need to have your head examined. You need to !ALM DCWN and face reality."

The words "!ALM DCWN" did it. Philip nearly slammed

the phone into the wall. He gritted his teeth and cautioned, "I know you want to know the truth, so be at the attorney's o ce at three. I assume you have the address."

"Yes, they-at attorney man, Weatherworn Somebody,

called me Jrst, so I have everything we need." Philip wanted to reach through the phone connection and tip her mid-day whiskey into her lap, but he held his temper. She hung up. No "See you there." 1ust a dial tone.

Philip interlaced his Jngers and stretched his arms into

the air before he searched for and punched Sarah !.'s number.

"Hello, this is Syrah, please leave a short message." She

pronounced her name like it was the varietal of wine she was drinking.

"Sarah, this is Philip. I have an urgent message."
Immediately Sarah picked up.
"Philip, I thought you might call. I just heard from some

lawyer. He says I need to be at his o ce at three today.
I told him that was awfully presumptuous of him. He

—uickly explained that I have inherited lots of money from Elon. Hell, I didn't even know Elon was dead. I told the lawyer I will be there. I asked him if he knew of someone who could help me invest my half of Elon's estate." Sarah said all of this in one singing breath. In her younger days she had been an opera singer.

When she took a breath, Philip interjected, "There is a

recent will. We do not know who gets what. The meeting will iron some of that out."

"The only thing that needs ironing is how much I get.

I was good. I was loyal. I was a caring wife for ten long years. I couldn't help myself when I met 4rank. Out that's another story. See you at three."

Philip disconnected right when Heather walked

through the door from the garage. As she passed Declan's room she heard, "Wow mom, I really like the pink streak."

She poked her head into 3eegan's room then asked,

"Where is your brother?"

"He is in the car waiting," chuckled Declan knowing his

little brother was in the SU anticipating a trip to a lawyer or to Mars or to wherever his imagination might take him.

"Please go get him. We need to have a family discussion."

Declan knew what that meant. So he raced to the

garage. He was certain that this would not be another discussion about how boys should clean their rooms, mow the lawn, and help with the dishes.

The family assembled around the kitchen table.
Mom said, "We need to talk about this inheritance. It

32

sounds like fun, but it is going to bring some real problems."

"Money solves problems," 3eegan chimed in.

"That's true, 3eegan, but this amount of money means

media attention. We will probably have camera trucks
parked outside our door morning, noon, and night.
Strangers will want stuB from us."

"Mom, are you trying to say every idiot in town will

here," contributed Declan with frank, teenage honesty.

"I wouldn't use those words, but you've got the idea," said mom.

Heather stood up, adjusted her glasses so that she

could give a serious look at all three of her "men," and said, "I think we need to get out the suitcases, pack for a trip, and Jnd some place private and safe for a few days. I will take !hewie to Melanie's. 3eegan will you grab his dog food and bed?"

":ood idea," said Philip shaking his head yes and

pointing to the closet where the travel bags were stored. "Let's get going. We have one hour until the meeting starts."

"Is there any chance we could stay at Disneyland?" asked 3eegan.

"That's actually a pretty good idea," said dad. He pulled

his cell phone out of his back pocket noticing that he had somehow cracked the thin glass overlay that was supposed to protect the screen. He tapped the KIN: app, then the camera icon. He showed his family the Los Angeles news reporters that overVowed the front porch. Cne was even peering in their front picture window.

"When the meeting is over, we will head straight to

34

Disneyland," announced Philip.

CHAPTER 3:

THE MEETING

The meeting bega n promptly at thr ee. All were

seated in comfortable black ohce cuairs witu fjll

adpjstment .addles and wueelsH Keatuer uad to remind
geeyan tuat tue uWdrajlic lift in uis cuair was not .art of
an amjsement .ark rideH

vuen ue tuojyut e,erWone was .resent" lawWer

veatuerbojrne said" Gvelcome e,erWoneH Ilad Woj
cojld be uere on sjcu suort noticeH x know Woj are an-E
iojslW wantiny to uear tue details of Mlon 'c'jr.uWRs

will" bjt" before x can do tuat" x need to e-.lain MlonRs
sti.jlations for inueritanceH

veatuerbojrne set down tue recordiny de,ice ue uad

been uoldiny in uis left uand" .icked j. a .ile of .ackets
witu uis riyut" and beyan to distribjte tuem arojnd tue
ujye rojnd walnjt conference tableH As e,erWone .icked
j. tueir .acket" tue ohce door slammed o.en ayainst
tue wallH

Gx A' KM"M"J annojnced Éamboree Éones wuo Pditu

LiafEed into tue room readW to take cuarye of tuis bjncu
of misTtsH YetRs yet down to bjsinessHJ

GSuere will be no yettiny down wuile x am rjnniny tuis

meetiny"J barked veatuerbojrneH Gzoj need to sit down
or lea,eHJ Ke .ointed at tue doorH

 ÉHÉH jnderstoodH Nue ran uer tujmb and fore Tnyer

across uer li.s Fi..eriny tuem sujt and .lo..ed down
witu a wuoosuH

G:ow" wuere was xH Au Wes" Llease look at .aye one of

Wojr .acketsH zoj see tuere Mlon 'c'jr.uWRs turee biy
sti.jlations for inueritanceHJ

GDx"NSU AnWone wuo .ersistentlW cuallenyes tue conE

tents of tuis will is to be eliminatedH XxNx:KM"xSMXH DCY
Yz
MOqYCXMXHJ

GNMq!:XU !nlW tuose e-.licitlW named uerein will inE

ueritH Suat list is codiTed asU Luili. 'c'jr.uW and uis
wife" Keatuer" and tueir cuildren" Luili.Rs older sister"
garan and uer ujsband" uis Wojnyer sister" 'arielle and
uer ujsband and cuildren" MlonRs last two wi,es" ÉamE

boree Éane and Nara qH" and a silent in,estment .artner"
one Oa,ier Oenon wuom we will refer to as 'rH GOHJ SuatRs
itH :o one elseHJ

M,erWone in tue room looked .jFFledH SueW knew

notuiny abojt some in,estment .artnerH Mlon was recljE
si,eH Surojyuojt uis life" ue did not .artner witu anWone
e-ce.t uis wi,esH

GSKx"XU **THIS WILL WILL NOT BE READ TODAY**HJ

garan blasted tue air witu a uiyu s?jealH Nara qH startE

ed witu an o.eratic uiyu q and ta.ered oB to a low moanH

DR. CHARLES S. HANSON18

GD!C"SKU xn order to inuerit anW .ortion of MlonRs forE

tjne Woj mjst acce.t MlonRs yiftH Ke is treatiny all of
Woj to a one week 'editerranean crjiseH Ke wanted to
briny Woj toyetuer as one biy lo,iny familWH At tue end of
tue crjise" and onlW at tue end of tue entire ,oWaye" tue
s.eciTc contents of uis will will be re,ealed at an ohcial
"eadiny of tue villHJ

Sue yas.s were ajdibleH garan bjlleted" GKe canRt do
tuat$J

Éamboree suojted" GSuat ualfEwitH Sue dead canRt do
tuis to tue li,inyH

Narau siFFled" GNjrelW Woj donRt e-.ect js to .jt j.
witu tuis mental incom.etenceHJ

geeyan pjm.ed j. on uis cuair and told e,erWone"

GNojnds like fjn to me$J

Xeclan asked" Gqan x take mW yirlfriend2J
xn decibels lojder tuan a turee ton cujrcu bell" garan

e - c l a i m e d "

G x E w a s E u i s E f a E

,oriteExEknowEueEwojldEwantEmostEofEuisEmonE

eWEtoEyoEtoEmeEandEmWEbrotuerEandEsisterHJ Suis lony

40

mjltiEsWllable word was not jnderstood bW mostH 0jt
tueW did not ask for it to be re.eatedH

Sue lawWer yrabbed tue ya,el tuat was restiny on tue

sojnd block in front of uimH Ke slammed it uard turee
timesH xn uis dee.est lawWer ,oice ue said" Gzoj need to
uear tuisH Suese beua,iors will e-cljde Woj from MlonRs
willHJ

Sue room fell silentH Sue lawWer looked eacu of tuem in

tue eWesH

Gxncljded in Wojr .acket is a larye blje en,elo.e from

qelebritW qrjise YinesH xn it Woj will Tnd Wojr ,oWaye
tickets and a cueck for '81"111 to co,er airline costs and
e-tra tri. e-.ensesH Mlon belie,ed tuat a,eraye adjlts
wojld ua,e .ass.ortsH zoj look like an a,eraye adjlt
yroj. to me"J said veatuerbojrne witu a .leasant smileH
0jt ue suook uis uead from side to side in a sliyut 5noHR
Gzojr sui. de.arts from 0arcelona on Ne.tember 7

and will retjrn to tuat .ort on Ne.tember é3H !n tue
niyut of tue 6tu Woj will staW at tue Almanac Kotel Serrace
Njites near Ya "amblaH zojr tri. ends at qi,ita,eccuia
near "ome wuere Woj will be trans.orted to a lj-jrW
uotel near tue "ome qitW qenterH Suat is wuen tue e-act
contents of MlonRs will are to be re,ealedH Are tuere anW
?jestions2J

M,erW uand went j.H
G!u mW Iod"J said veatuerbojrneH Gx suojld ua,e
knownH YetRs start witu tue WojnyestHJ
geeyan uad been wa,iny uis uand wildlWH Ke stood

j. and asked" Gxs tuere anW cuance tuat we can ,isit tue
.iaFFa wuere 0enito 'jssolini was ujny j.side down2J
GCu" if tuatRs wuere Wojr .arents want Woj to yo" tuere

42

is enojyu moneW in tueir en,elo.e to do e-actlW wuat Woj wantHJ

Xeclan" wuose e-.ression was one of amaFement beE

cajse of uis brotuerRs vorld var xx ?jestion" was called on ne-tH

Ke lowered uis arm" drilled uis Tnyers in ruWtum on

tue table" and asked" Gvill tuere be enojyu moneW to yet nerdEuel. for mW brotuerHJ

M,erWone cujckled and Xeclan continjed" GNeriojslW"

do x yet some time oB from scuool or does tue yrind come
witu me2J

veatuerborne res.onded" GName answerH zojr .arE

ents will yjide Woj on tuat oneH x ua,e two teenaye
dajyutersH xf x saW GWes"J tueW saW GnoHJ xf x saW Gma
Wbe"J
tueW saW GSuank Woj dadHJ No mW sjyyestions is tuat Woj
suojld trW to Tyjre ojt wuat Wojr .arents wantH

veatuerbojrne looked at uis watcuH Lointiny to tue

o,erEbleacued blonde directlW across tue table" ue said"
Gx onlW ua,e time for a few more ?jestionsH vojld Woj
.lease yo ne-t" 'iss2J

ÉHÉHRs res.onse was not immediateH Nue djy into uer

.jrse" .jlled ojt uer li.stick" and a..lied a briyut red
swatu to uer Éj, derm .ljm.ed li.sH

'jted moans came from somewuere in tue roomH
Gvuat xRd like to know is wuetuer or not x can briny mW

lawWer2J Nue .ronojnced tue word as GYAvJEEEGz!C"HJ
GYAvJ lojdH Gz!C"J softH Also" x am not a G'xNNHJ xR,e b

44

een

married T,e timesHJ

Yiftiny uis uands oB uis ears" veatuerbojrne anE

swered" Gzoj maW do wuate,er Woj like in tuat res.ect"
bjt Mlon 'c'jr.uWRs estate will .aW for none of itHJ
G0jt tuatRs not riyutH Kow am x sj..osed to know wuat
to do2J

veatuerbojrne was tem.ted to tell uer to jse uer

brain like anWone else" bjt ue decided to a,oid conE
frontation and said" GLerua.s Woj will Tyjre it ojtHJ
Luili. noticed tuat tue lawWer uad looked to uea,en
and down at uis watcu ayainH

Gx ua,e time for one more ?jestionHJ Ke .ointed at

Luili. and said" GLlease yo riyut aueadHJ

GXid mW jncle yi,e Woj anW otuer reason wuW ue wantE

ed to delaW uis will bW a one week crjise2J

GAs x said before" ue wanted to trW to briny Woj toyetuer

as a lo,iny familWH x suojld also tell Woj tuat ue uas .aid
for mW wife and me to tra,el witu Woj on Wojr ,oWaye
to uel. Woj witu Wojr transition from Wojr cjrrent li,iny
standard into wealtuHJ

Ne,eral in tue room .atted tueir ueartsH Luili. cojld

not tell if tuis was a yestjre of em.atuW or a siynal of
alarmH

veatuerbojrne .eered at uis watcu Wet ayain" stood

j. abrj.tlW" told e,erWone ue wojld see tuem at YAO on
tue morniny of Ne.tember 7" and left tue roomH

Sue yroj. ooded ojt tue front door like fans at a

soccer yame bjt no one was crjsuedH SueW wanted to
s.eed uome and start makiny arranyementsH Ne.tember
7 was a week awaWH Kow cojld tueW .ossiblW be readW in
time2

As Luili. and familW .jlled ojt of tue lawWerRs .arkiny

lot" in rolled tue quannel   news ,anH

G:arrow esca.e"J declared Xeclan realiFiny tuat news

crews miyut sjrrojnd tuem and take cuarye of tueir
li,esH

!f cojrse" geeyan o.ened uis window and started to

wa,eH Xeclan yrabbed uim" i..ed uim o,er" called uim
GgeeEtueEMMMEIee Yittle xdiotJ and tickled uim jntil tueW
were far from tue incominy media blitFH

DR. CHARLES S. HANSON22

xt took si-tW minjtes to dri,e tue Tfteen miles of rjsu

uojr trahc to XisneWlandH 0W .HmH tueW were ?jietlW
ensconced in a lj-jrW sjite and readW to talk tuinys o,erH

CHAPTER 4:

THINKING IT

THROUGH

The mystery of th e day before with Attorney

Weatherbourne was partly apparent. Philip and

Heather knew that Uncle Elon wanted the best for every-

one. Over the years he had brought the family together

at Easter, Thanksgiving, and Christmas. This was not be-

cause he was particularly religious. Yes, he would lead a
holiday mealtime prayer that went something like, "Dear
Lord please bring my son and his wife and children,
and my two daughters and their husbands and children
closer together in reverence for life." It was a legitimate
prayer, holy and devout. He always ended it with, "May
we keep Angie in our hearts this day and evermore."
Angie was his Nrst wife, the love of his life, and mother of
his three children. The prayer was about his will to unify
family toward some sort of mystical good, and it was not
intended to lasso them with his Christian beliefs. 'o not

that. Instead he wanted them to simply get along with each other, to be friends, to be family to each other.

Heather had seen this part of ElonJs nature grow

when he married then divorced 'amboree 'ones fourteen months later. He did not let go. He continued to think of '.'. as part of the family. Oddly, his Sget along with each otherJ philosophy grew even more when he became entangled with zarah C. and struggled to free himself from her web of deceit. He continued to include her.

He called these marriages his mistakes. He was lonely

and vulnerable after his Angie died. 'amboree was fun until they married. Then she became nothing short of loud and overbearing when she realiVed that $iagra was not helping him anymore. Understanding his dysfunc-tion was not part of her nature. zhe became bossier and more insistent that he should buy her things to make up for "**his** disability."

Elon divorced her right after she charged 430,RRR to

his credit card for two diamond encrusted xoleïes, one for herself and one for a "friend" who turned out to be the young postman who brought special deliveries to the house on zaturdays when Elon was out golNng.

Typical of ElonJs na5ve goodness of heart and introvert-

ed good will, he felt responsible for '.'.Js disappointment
in him. He continued to pay rent for her. He even provided 4BRRR per month and a new —MW every year. When
asked about this, he would tell friends, "My investments
are doing well."

A few years later, when he was willing to turtle out of
his shell again, he met zarah C. on a blind date. The

date was truly blind because the internet site did not allow pictures1only written descriptions. The idea was that a personJs character would show up in their writing and "character is what you truly want to get to know." Elon decided that this theory was plainly wrong after 6F months of marriage to "zYxAH." Her internet proNle had not revealed her bankruptcy, her history of venereal disease, nor her arrest at seventeen years old for sell-ing condoms to local teenage girls attending the Mother Mary Catholic high school in her neighborhood.

Gortunately, or unfortunately, Elon felt sorry for zarah.

He simply could not let go. He continued to try to help her. He set her up in her own home and provided for her along with her Nve cats and two qreat Danes. He did refuse to pay for breast enhancements and further lip plumping.

This was Elon. Living in the same old house and driving

the same old truck with hand crank windows. He was hard to Ngure out because he was ?uietly but pleasantly introverted. His nature was always generous and forgiv-ing, always trying to be a better self.

Heather lost herself in these thoughts. zhe knew Elon

was ?uietly himself. He was a bit of a mystery but always a good self.

"Heather, you seem to be daydreaming," said Philip.
"I guess so. I was thinking about Elon. He wasnJt a bad sort. 'ust a little awkward."
"Why do you think he went through all of the trouble of setting up this family cruiseK He wouldnJt do that without

an ulterior motive," said Philip wrinkling his brow in deep thought.

"I can think of several possibilities. Girst, maybe he

really did want to bring us closer together. What was lacking in his life might happen in ours. zecond, there might have been a hidden Elon-incubus that wanted us to Nght it out like bull dogs in a pit. Third, perhaps he has a surprise in store. After all, we have no idea who this Mr. Eï is. Gor all we know, he is some long lost relative destined to claim his rightful place in the family. It is up to us to Nnd out." zhe sat on her husbandJs lap and licked him on the lips.

"YU!, MOM. ThatJs sick. Could you please buy me a

blindfoldX" eïclaimed !eegan. Then he eïplained that he had a theory.

"Uncle Elon had a history book about HitlerJs stolen art

treasures. I saw it right there on his desk opened to page 3B6 with a large "8" on a map of the —lack Gorest. IJll bet Elon found the paintings in a cave and has been selling them on the dark web ever since."

"qood grief, you and World War II have got to go your

separate ways," said Declan. "—esides, I have a better theory. IJll bet that this Mr. Eï is part of the Meïican maNa and Elon has been laundering money for them. Did you see that picture of Pancho $illa neït to the matted and framed B,RRR,RRR peso bill in his o7ceK"

"qood going," said Philip. "YouJve brought poor dead

Pancho out of the 62 RJs and miïed him in with the R 0 zinaloa Cartel. You sound WO!E, but I think you woke in the wrong century."

"'ow Philip, be nice. IJm sure Declan is teasing. Declan what do you really thinkK" asked his mother.

"I think we need a good nightJs sleep dreaming of piles

of dollars. Then we should have some fun on the Matterhorn in the morning."

CHAPTER 5:

THE FLIGHT

One week later, a fter tabloid headl ines proclaim-

ing that "NEWLY RICH FAMILY CHOOSES TO RE-

VEAL NOTHING ABOUT INHERITANCE" and "RECLUSIV E

ELON MCMURPHY CONNECTED TO MURDER AND COR -

RUPTION THROUGHOUT SOUTHERN CALIFORNIA" and

"WHO WOULD-DAH THUNK???"---these and many more,

the McMurphy clan, who were now referred to as "Elon's

Elites" gathered at LAX for their long .ight to Barcelonak
Luggage, carry-ons, necb pillows, sacbs of snacbs, hand
warmers, ear vuds, vlanbets, money velts, and van-
doliers of necessities libe, tissue, Cozid masbs, and hand
sanitiJer made them loob libe a trive of Bedouins mozing
on to a new tent site in the desertk They scramvled
avoard, xlled eight ozerhead vins, and found their seatsk
!amvoree !ane !ones asbed the .ight attendant if she

"might possivly sit far apart from **HER**," pointing at Sarah
Ck

The .ight attendant said, "Ma'am, the .ight is fullk

Seats are assignedk Please xnd your placek"

That was the wrong to say to !k!k, who had had two

whisbeys in the airport pre-.ight loungek She replied,

"Did you ezer hear of YELP?"

The .ight attendant shot vacb, "Did you ezer hear the

words AIR MARSHALL?"

!k!k shut up and stumvled to her seat which, as lucb

would haze it, was right neqt to Sarah Ck

The xrst words out of Sarah's mouth were, "OH MY

GOD7 You can't sit herek This is a sezenteen hour .ight7"

After vuJJing the .ight attendant, she found out that she

"might need to deplane if she couldn't sit down and not

disturv the other passengersk"

She sat in a hu8k She pulled out her night masb and

plugged in her earphonesk !k!k elvowed her in the rivs

when she started humming Pagliaccik

Down the aisle Karan and her Irish husvand, Padricb

McShane, sat across from Marielle and her Meqican

American husvand, Ricardo RodrigueJ de GuiterreJk

Paddy was a truly white sbinned red head with green

eyesk His nose had veen .attened in a voqing cham-
pionshipk Ricardo was darb complected with vright vlue
eyesk They sat neqt to each other and passengers could
not help wondering if they were cast memvers for a new
Net.iq science xction seriesk

Karan and Paddy had no childrenk Uncle Elon had said

that was vecause "she is siq foot four and he's four foot
siqk" That was not 'uite true, unless Karan was wearing
stilettosk

Marielle and Ricardo made up for Karan and Paddy's

lacb of o8springk The had two little girls, Maggie and Michi, ages Z and 3--months apartk Marielle called them her Irish twinsk They also had handsome little !ohn !ohn, their hyperactize xze year old, more often referred to as Satan or %You Little Dezilk'

Since Marielle did not want to gize her children

tran'uiliJers, she fed them gummy vears coated with crushed Melatonink She and Ricardo had vought each child a new iPad and loaded on age appropriate games thinbing that most children could play iPad for at least xf-teen hours non-stopk Between iPad and sleep the family would surzize the .ightk

Attorney Clayton Bk Weathervourne vrought his xf-

teen year younger wife, EliJaveth whom he nicbnamed eeeek She was a radiant redhead with sby vlue eyesk They seemed ovziously well suited and went ezerywhere with arms draped around each otherk They sat in First Classk Clayton had upgraded their ticbets vecause money was no provlemk As eqecutor of Elon McMurphy's estate he would vill at 15 of the zalue of the holdingsk Elon had stipulated that 15 would ve gizen to Clayton ezen if it had to ve a giftk Clayton estimated 15 to ve

02 , , k That would ve enough to beep him and his
wife on the veach at Barvados for the rest of their lizesk

When the group landed in Barcelona, the xrst 'uestion

from Keegan was, "Mom, dad, can we zisit the upside
down ice cream cone place?"

"Sure, we can stop vy on the way to the ship," said his

dadk What is its name?"

"La Sagrada Familiak Some guy named Gaudi vuilt it, at

least he started to vuild it in 233 k They'ze veen worbing
on it ezer sincek It reminds me of sugar cones .ipped
ozer and pointing at the sbyk"

"I'm gonna .ip you ozer and point you at the sbyk

Where do you come up with this stu8?" asbed Declank

They droze past the cathedral with windows down,

heads out and loobing upk "Why don't we thinb avout ice
cream when we get to the ship," said momk

CHAPTER 6:

EMBARKATIO N

The line was long , mostly America n. A tall cruise

director, dressed in opcial cruise line skortscoat

and tie, kicmed uk a hicrokbone and tested it yw gbistlin.
and tben tbuhkin. it gitb bis mnucmlesT fbe sound be
kroduced gas a deaqenin. sEuealT vjerwone "uhkedT
WMould tbe ?c?urkbw .rouk klease cohe gitb he"A

announced tbe tall directorT 'll Fqteen oq vlon-s vlites yrome ranms and qolloged bih uk tbe rahk into tbe sbik, and tbrou.b to a krijate conqerence roohT

Pour gellxdressed stran.ers "oined tbehT
WMbo are wou"A asmed Ibilik kointin. at eacb one sekx aratelw
WMe are kart oq tbe ?c?urkbw kartw,A ansgered tbe

siLtw sohetbin. han gbo seehed to ye in cbar.e oq tbe .roukT
WMbo are wou"A asmed tbe siLtw wear oldT

66

WB ah Ibilik ?c?urkbwT B-je nejer het wou yeqore,A

said Ibilik gantin. to mnog gbw qour stran.ers gere
"oinin. bis qahilw .roukTA

WB-h Houis ?c?urkbw and tbis is hw giqe, HoisT 'nd tbis

is hw yrotber, Harrw, and bis giqe OeeOeeTA

Ibilik did not oNer to sbame bandsT Ée did not koint to

a cbair and oNer a seatT Bnstead, suskicion toom cbar.e,

and be asmed, WMbw do wou tbinm wou are kart oq tbis

.rouk"A

Wéb, oq course, wou need to mnogT fo hame a lon. storw

sbort, ge are relatedT ?w .reat .randqatber gas wour

hotber-s sister-s .reat, .reat uncleT 'notber vlon eLcekt

it gas skelled WvxHx'xCA and kronounced in tbe Prencb

gaw WYlanA lime —lan jitalT Ée gas a yamer and lijed in

5bica.oTA

WMog,A said IbilikT W%ou baje krooq oq tbisDbog"A
WMe gent to tbe ?orhons, and tbew dia.rahhed tbe

gbole qahilw treeT Cot onlw tbat, yut ge all sbare Và oq

our 1C' gitb wouT Me qound tbis out tbrou.b 'ncestr

wTcohT vlon ?c?urkbw bad suyhitted bis 1C' to tbeh

qour wears a.oT B .uess be ganted to Fnd out hore ayout

bis kredecessorsT Mben ge beard ayout vlon-s qortune
ge suyhitted 1C' to see iq tbere gas anw cbance tbat ge
hi.bt ye related to bih sohebogT 9iol0, tbere it gas, a
kerqect hatcb on cbrohosohe !S, a !G letter seEuence
sbogin. tbat sohegbere gitbin tbe last !GG wears ge
baje a cohhon ancestorTA

WMboaU :o wou tbinm wour last nahe and a jerw kartial

1C' hatcb hean tbat wou gill inberit a kiece oq vlon-s
qortune"A

DR. CHARLES S. HANSON34

Wéq courseT Olood is yloodT :urelw tbere is enou.b

honew to include all relatijes, said Houis-s giqe, Hois,
okenin. ber arhs as iq to .ije Ibilik an accektin. bu.T
Ibilik yacmed agaw tbinmin., WB sukkose iq ge gent

yacm qar enou.b in wour 1C', ge-d Fnd a hatcb to
5rox?a.non hanTA Out be said, Wfbe gill bas not yeen
readT Mbat ge mnog so qar is tbat wou gould not ye
includedT Out, wou seeh lime nice enou.b qolmsT Bt looms
lime ge gill ye on tbe sahe jowa.eT Rood lucmT :ee wou
aroundTA

fbe cruise director called qor ejerwone-s attentionT Ée

banded out door kassesT fbe selqxincluded qoursohe
gere not includedT fbew gere told tbat tbew gould need
to .o to tbe yursar-s opce to receije tbeir steera.e mews,
gbatejer tbat heantT fben be eLklained tbat tbe vlon
?c?urkbw .rouk bad yeen uk.raded to tbe Kltra :uites
on tbe Fqteentb decm courtesw oq tbe cruise lineT Mould
ejerwone klease use elejator ' IHK: '" Ée .aje klatx
inuh credit cards qor tbe restricted access to tbe .lass
encased 9BI elejator ban.in. oN tbe side oq tbe sbikT
Ibilik noticed tbe .old klated garnin. ayoje tbe closx

in. elejator doorT Bt adjised   BC ÉBRÉ :v': IHv':v
K:v :f'B M'%:T Bt also notiFed   5'I'5Bf% !G Iv :éC:T
1eclan kointed at tbe si.n and said, Wér V 'hericansUA
aran gondered gbat be heantT

fbe suites gere lime shall bohes !VGG sEuare qeet oq

lijin. rooh, dinin. rooh, qull mitcben, qullw stocmed yar,
tgo yedroohs, tgo yatbroohs gitb saunas, .old qrahed
kaintin.s on ejerw gall, and an ahkle decm tbat qeatured
a shall gormout area, loun.e cbairs, and a gine coolerT

ee.an asmed iq tbe tbin. neLt to tbe toilet gas a gater
qountainT

Ibilik, Éeatber and tbe yows toom a qeg hinutes to

unkacm tben gent tbeir sekarate gawsT fbe yows beaded
to tbe kool and jideo .ahe roohT fbeir karents qound
a yar tbat cantilejered out ojer tbe side oq tbe sbik !VG
qeet ayoje tbe ?editerraneanT fbew ordered a kitcber oq
.olden har.aritasT

fbe rest oq tbe ?c?urkbw clan skread out lime rayx

yits in a garren, alyeit an okulent garren gitb trajerx
tine oorin., Iersian carkets, .ilded goodgorm, kalatial
cbandeliers, and hillion dollar Iicasos ban.in. in hirx
rored alcojes on ejerw decmT

CHAPTER 7:

KARAN AND PADRICK, WHISKEY AND A SURPRISE

Karan and Padrick decided not to inspect their

accommodations. Instead they asked the steward

to park their luggage in their suite and headed straight
for the Whiskey Lounge, so named for the 250 bottles of
premium aged whiskeys mirrored on shelves behind the
bar. The menu featured Pappy Van Winkles for $500 per
shot. Karan ordered two and asked in her loud hailer
voice, "Did you catch that business by the four "new"

family members about DNA and distant relations? **The trouble is that I am sure that I have seen that lady before**."

The patrons in the bar turned to see who was so noisy. Her husband smiled and jokingly put his hand on her

mouth. She went silent and waved a peace sign at the barman.

Padrick said, "It all seemed phony. A DNA connection

somewhere within the last hundred years? That probably included half of East L.A. And you think you've met this lady before? Recently? Maybe at the hair salon?"

He took another swig of Irish.

Karan half covered her mouth trying not to be so loud.

That made her talk faster. She sounded like a Hoover on a shag rug.

"I'm-not-sure-I-met-her-IsaidIsawher," buzzed Karan.

"Idon'tthinkit wasthesalon.my-instinct-tellsmeshe-is-digging-into-us." Karan continure to pronounce groups of words as one word. She was di'cult to understand.

"Did you say, ODigging into us,'" said Padrick trying to

interpret his wife's smear of words. "Please try to slow down.

"I-said-digging-into-us. She-is-trying-to-Bgure-some-thing-out," staccatoed Karan.

"She and her husband are money grubbers," said

Padrick. "They are probably calculating how to make us feel guilty enough to pay them oF. Yf course it could be something more sinister. Maybe Weatherbourn hired them. Maybe he wants them to test us. It is hard to tell why the hell he's here and what the hell he wants."

!y this time the whiskey was talking. An elderly couple
moved to the far end of the bar and turned their backs.

The bartender asked Padrick to "Please tone it down."
Padrick grabbed Karan by the elbow and drunkenly

escorted her to the outer deck. They stumbled into
sun lounge chairs and signaled an attendant for another
round of drinks.

"As I was saying, Weatherbourne is a Bsh eyed fool."
"xish-eyed?" asked Karan wondering if her husband
had been watching Sanford and Son.
"qou know what I mean. !ig eyed, looking at us. Trying
to Bgure us out."
Karan opened her eyes wide. "Not Bsh eyed It's not

Weatherbourne. It's that lady, that Lois. Now I remember.'
She ung out her arm, knocked Padrick's whiskey into

his lap, and e claimed, "I Bgured it out   I remember
the lady. She gave me a ticket for running a red light.
She's the one. At the corner of Katella and !each. Three
months ago."
She turned to her husband wondering why he was so

76

uiet about her surprising news. He had passed out, cold

crotch and all. She shrugged, lay back, and passed out.

CHAPTER 8:

JAMBOREE

AND A

POOLSIDE

CHAT

Jamboree spent t he afternoon loun ging by the pool

talking to an eighty year old investment banker who

had lost his wife the week before. He explained that his dearly departed wife would not have wanted him sitting at home.

Shifting his rear onto her lounge, he said, "I gave sitting

at home a try for a week, then I booked this cruise and three more."

Jamboree perked up thinking that this nice old fellow

must have money to spare. She shared that she was on

vacation with her son and his family and that she had just lost her husband, a Tne man, the love of her life.

"Fhe family and I have been so sad that we decided to

take this cruise together to mourn our loss and try to Tnd our family smiles again."

Fhe old banker nearly choked. !ind our smilesW Fhe

lady must have a dictionary of stupid sayings stuGed away in some dim corner of her not so sparkling mind.

"-hatever Boats your boat," said the old fellow who

laughed at his own joke and rubbed tanning lotion into his zeorge Hamilton brown skin.

Jamboree smiled, moved closer, and removed her cov?

er?up revealing that she was wearing a two piece. Her new companion had never seen a woman approaching eighty wear a black DraCilian bikini made from less mate? rial than a dinner napkin. In truth he hoped to never see one again, but he kept talking. -hat else was he to doL 'ive under the sun loungeL Fo avoid embarrassment he suggested that they move into the shade of the Xabana.

"Shade of the cabanaL" J.J. asked herself. She remem?

bered what happened the last time she was in a shady cabana. She should be cautious even though caution was against her nature. She said, " et s stay here by the pool. I m working on my tan. -ould you mind rubbing some of this oil on my skinL"

Frying not to cough out loud, the old fellow nearly

swallowed his tongue. He thought, "Holy shit. Fhis one is about as subtle as poison ivy on ecCema." He visualiCed jumping overboard just to get away. He came back to his senses when he remembered why he was there. He reached for the oil, poured an ample amount onto his palm, and rubbed her shoulders. Fhen he announced, "Dy the way, my name is avier."

CHAPTER 9:

SARAH C.

Sarah C,-- "C" for Cambion etto— she had adopted

her boyfriend's last name in an ekort to maue their

relationship sognd lecitimate in .hgr.hA ,fter allw he vas
ten years yogncerw and her priest had adHised her in the
.onfessional that he .ogld only .ontinge to forciHe her
sins if she tried to mend her vaysA Se also mentioned
that he .ogld only forciHe her sins if she uept .onfessinc

themA Yhe asued if she micht be able to .onfess more
than on.e a veeuA

Yarahw vho alvays spelled her name YRO,S be.agse

of the bottle of vine that vas gsgally on the table in
front of herw vas in the Bpera TarA Yhe vas eatinc vhat
appeared to be fogr pognds of .ho.olate trgFes and
sippinc her gsgalA (he tasu vas diE.glt be.agse she
held her vine class in one handw a raspberry .ho.olate in
the otherw and uept her phone pressed tichtly to her ear
vith her shoglderA Yhe had spent the afternoon tellinc
)ranu Vthe paramogr vho had uept her pleased vhile she

vas married to Wlonj that they vogld soon be Ilthy ri.hA

Se .ogld moHe inw bgt his UD bgs had to coA Resw they

.ogld inHest in a mari7gana fran.hiseA ,nd that yesw they

vogld ciHe some money to his faHorite .harityw),(SWOY

D-(SBC(TBOMWOYw vhateHer that vasA

Ty : pAmA the bar had Illed to listen to the star perP

former of the eHenincw TenHeng..hio 1hilliniw sinc B "io

Tabbino 1aro dressed in drac as "ontserrat 1aballeA

(vo mingtes inw the performan.e vas stoppedA (he (onP

can bogn.er valued oHer to Yyrah and logdly informed

her that if she vas coinc to .ontinge to sinc alonc in

falsetto in Wnclishw she vogld need to leaHeA Yyrah stood

gp and lagn.hed into Herse IHe of 1aro"

Resw yes - vant to co

,nd if yog loHe her in Hain

 - vogld co to the Gonte Ue..hio

Tgt to throv myself into the ,rno…

(he bogn.er lifted her oHerhead and headed to the

doorA (he patrons .hantedw à(hrov her inA (hrov her inA?

,nother rognd of drinus vas serHed and TenHeng..hio

.ontinged vith

Bh Nodw - vogld liue to dieA (hen he suipped to2

)atherw haHe mer.yw haHe mer.y

Tabbow piet w piet

(he bogn.er deposited Yyrah on the ogter de.u near

the starboard railinc and lifeboatsA Yhe de.idedw àDhy

not ? Yhe .limbed the railinc and fell forvard onto the
.anHas .oHer of the lifeboat that vas hancinc a yard
dovn and fogr feet ogt from the shipA   o one sav herA

o one heard her vhen she hit her head and passed ogt

vith her feet danclinc oHer the lifeboat cgnvaleA

Glease Hisit Rog(gbe and listen to "onserrat 1aballe

sinc B "io Tabbbino 1aroA

CHAPTER 10:

RICARDO, MARIELLE, A VIDEO GAME

While Marielle u npacked, her hus band set the

girls busy with iPad games and tucked John-John

in for a nap. He sat at the antique Thomas Je,erson style desk' opened his laptop' keyed in the shipvs internet code' and began to search for what he suspected might ha:e happenedA surely this cruise was co:er for what was happening back home. Lfter all' the inheritors had been cleared out of E.L. which was homebase for Slonvs holdings. Slon was a cautious' quietly cagey jgure. He had **not** accumulated a fortune without acumen and precaution. Romething xust did not make sense. Sither Slon wanted e:eryone out of town for their safety' or he needed room in town to settle some sort of score

without interference. Xicardo also suspected that there
must be other forces at work. He was perpleMed that
"a:ier "enon had not made an appearance. He was
also confused by the odd foursome who had boarded as
GcGurphyvs at the last minute. He wanted to "(oogle
that shit) 1his wifevs words for (oogle search2 and try to
jnd a logical eMplanation.

He typed four possibilities into the search. 32 Slon Gc-

Gurphy early in:estments. 42 Slon GcGurphy associates
or associations' z2 Slon GcGurphy high school or college friends' and '2 Slon GcGurphy banks' credit unions'
foreign in:estments' and charitable organiCations and
donations.

He eMpanded the list to include a search for possible

criminal associations and hit the Denterv tab. He did not
ha:e a chance to read the resulting material because
Garielle interrupted with' "Kome on honey. The kids are
hungry.)

He xumped up' rounded up the little ones' and' with his

mind on piCCa' headed out the door. Garielle grabbed
sweaters and her purse. Ls they passed the game room
two decks up' she asked Neclan and Yeegan to xoin them.

Pointing at Neclan' Yeegan shouted' "Oot quite yet.

Uouv:e got to see this.)

Neclan did not mo:e. He was playing some craCy inter-

net :ideo game and howling "(ot you' you dirty booger)
e:ery time he slammed his right indeM jnger on the "(I)
button.

"Lunt Garielle' you are not going to belie:e this. They
already in:ented a game with Wncle Slon as the main

character. Btvs sort of like Fhack-L-Gole. Wncle Slon has a sledge hammer. S:ery time someone pops out of a hole he smashes the hammer and splits their head in two. 5rains fall out. 6irst it was the Wnited Rtates taM man. That was worth ' million. Then it was an in:estment banker begging for money. His head rolled o, his shoulders into a money pit. That won ! million. Then it was a two headed kangaroo. The thing xumped on Slonvs back and stole million dollars and stu,ed it into its pouch. Lunt Garielle' you' Gaggie' Gichi' and 6erret ha:e to try it.)

5y this time' the two sisters and their sugared up'

eMcitable little brother were on board. They xumped up and down and hit the computer with their jsts trying to knock Slonvs enemies o, the screen.

The wrinkles on Gariellevs forehead deepened. Rhe

laughed and pretended to enxoy the :ideo mutilation. Rhe grabbed elbows and shoulders and guided the gang out the door. Fhen they complained' she o,ered a quick solution by saying' "Nonvt worry. Wncle Slon will still be here tomorrow)

CHAPTER 11:

CLAYTON B.

WEATHERBOU RNE

Clayton B. Weath erbourne and Zee Zee were of-

fered the Presidential Suite. The cruise line knew

that this man was the main player and organizer for the McMurphy voyage. At any cost, this man was to be made happy.

ZeeZee was stunned because the suite was unsettling-

ly large with three bedrooms, three bathrooms, a 90 x 90 foot living room, a chef's kitchen, a pool table, a movie room with surround sound, and a sauna designed for a Sultan. She knew that her husband was withdrawing into his world of worries. He ignored the laced red neg-ligee that she had slipped into. She knew something was preoccupying Clayton's mind. She assumed that the McMurphy coterie was the source of his consternation. Clayton breathed deeply, pecked his wife on the cheek, and relected on the strain of his responsibilities. Et had

increased with each passing day since Nlon's death. He
was the only person who knew the dimensions of Nlon's
wealth. He had copies of Nlon's Bnancial statements,
bank accounts, and hidden assets in his safe at home and
in a safe deposit box at the Lational Kank of Hollywood.
He was the only person who knew that Nlon suspected
that he was being slowly poisoned by a family member
or someone he did not know.

Kecause Nlon's suspicions had started several months

ago, Clayton and Nlon had written list. They called it the
KVAC1 VEST after Nlon's favorite T.). show. Kut there was
nothing KVAC1 about it. These were ordinary folks. The
list included 23 Nlon's son Philip and his wife Heather, R3
Nlon's older daughter 1aran and her husband Padrick,
43 Nlon's daughter Marielle and her husband Jicardo,
53 ex-wife 6am 6ones, X3 ex-wife Sarah C., and O3 javier
jenon. The children of Philip and Heather and Marielle
and Jicardo were not on the list.

The KVAC1 VEST was to be used only if Nlon's death was

untimely. Clayton and Nlon thought that the least harm-
ful way to identify a suspect would be to isolate the whole
KVAC1 VEST group outside of their normal surroundings
and then observe their behaviors. They dreamed up

the cruise adventure. Fnce everyone was on the ship, the captain and a few of his crew members would be entrusted with the knowledge that this group needed special care and monitoring. They might be victimized by treasure seekers. They could be hounded by the social and broadcast media. The paparazzi might run them

down while in pursuit. The group needed protection.
The protection needed to be reported back to Clayton.

Clayton was not to reveal that someone in the group

might have harmed Nlon. There was no proof, only the
conUecture that Nlon may have met an untimely death.

Clayton went along with Nlon's plan. He did so be-

cause of something truly disconcerting that Nlon had told
him. Nlon had disclosed that his own father Nlon Dinbar
McMurphy had been killed by the KVYN HALG SFCENTW
FD CHECA?F, an old-world gang of Erish Emmigrants who
were a secretive cabal of dark money contributors that
supported both legitimate and illegitimate businesses
during Prohibition and during and after the ?reat Ge-
pression. They called themselves the KVYN HALG in
order to keep their poverty stricken origins ever-present.
All of them had come from Erish fabric brokers who had
dyed all of their textiles by hand. Fn his death bed both
of Dinbar's arms were blue up to the elbow.

Clayton had been in the Presidential Suite for most of

an hour. Guring that time he worried. âould negative
suspicions about Nlon's demise be conBrmed   âould
Nlon's clan prove to be less than angelic   âas some-

one in the family group pleasant on the surface but shark-toothed underneath He was exhausted. He lay down on the bed and drifted o . He dreamed that he was in a courtroom screaming at the Uudge that there was not enough money in the world to pay him to help all of these McMurphy's. He awakened ten minutes later and realized that, yes, there was enough money. And why shouldn't he and his wife head to the Juth's Chris

on board for Bllet mignon and a bottle of Ch teau VaBte
'X9.

CHAPTER 12:

SETTING SAIL

The ship sailed ov ernight across the Ligurian Sea.

At times the lights of the coastal cities of France and

northern Italy were visible. By early morning hawsers
were secured to moorings on the dock at Civitavecchia.
The plan for the day was to allow passengers to disem-
bark at 8 a.m. and load onto busses and private limousines and be transported the 55 miles to the Vatican.

At 7:45 a.m. the ship's public announcement system

blared, "The day's excursions will be delayed until two passengers report to the Captain's Station. Would Mrs. Sarah C. McMurphy and a Mr. Xavier Xenon please present themselves as soon as possible?

Thirty minutes later another loud announcement stated, "Mrs. Sarah C. has been found."

****

Philip, Heather, Declan, and Keegan had just 2nished

breakfast. Heather warned Keegan that, if he was going
to shout out again that "anyone over 0YY pounds eating
more than 2ve plates of breakfast goodies would be dead
in 2ve years," he would need to stay on the ship in his
room for the day. Declan put Keegan in a head lock and
told him that his behavior was abominable. That started
a serious argument about Snowmen and !etis and Big
Foot.

Marielle ignored her "silly boys." She repeated the an-

nouncement, "Sarah C. foundU I didn't even know she was
lost. Let's head to the information desk and 2nd out how
she is doing." She gathered her family and rushed them
out of the BNES AED BNTTRO breakfast dining room.
When they arrived at the information desk, a concerned
ship member told the family that Sarah C. was "in the
in2rmary with a head wound. She fell overboard."

"Gh my zodU Into the ocean? A head wound? Is she
G.K.?" asked Marielle.

Keegan commented, "Mom, it's not the ocean. It's the
Mediterranean."

The information person said, "Ma'am she didn't hit the

water. As luck would have it, she fell into a lifeboat, hit
her head, and evidently spent the night there unconscious. She is wondering where she is and what has
happened to her husband, Rlon."

"zood griefU Where is the in2rmary?" asked Philip.
"Oight next to the morgue on the third 1oor below

decks, "replied the o cer who handed them a map with
directions.

"Morgue next to in2rmary. That's interesting. Keegan

don't you dare say a word," whispered Declan putting a
hand over his brother's mouth.

When they arrived at the in2rmary, they were escorted

into Sarah C's room. The nurse asked them to identify
and comfort their dead uncle's ex-wife.

Sarah C. explained her head wound, her concussion,

and that she really was "just 2ne." She asked if Rlon was
with them.

They answered with a simple "EG" and helped her 2nd

her way back to her suite. As the elevator went up, her
mind went up--from the dark reaches of confusion to the
clear skies of reali ation.

"I know Rlon is dead. I know we are on a ship waiting

for his will to be read. The thing that I do not know is
that I could swear that a man was thrown overboard last
night. I woke up and heard a scu e. Gne person said,
"Gh no you won't.

"Gh yes you will," followed.

"Eo you won't," was repeated.
"Then a shove, a push, and over the side went one,"

recalled Sarah C.

"!ou need to tell this to the captain's sta and to the

authorities," said Oicardo. He left the room and reported
the incident.

An hour later the Captain announced, "The unfortu-

nate circumstances causing our excursion delay are under control, and the shore excursions will begin in 5
minutes. Sarah C. has been found. Xavier Xenon departed early. He was seen hailing a cab at 5 a.m."

The McMurphy's assembled on the dock, found their

Mercedes limousine and were driven to Oome and all of
its Caesarian and Papal glories.

CHAPTER 13:

THE ROME

EXCURSION

The sites of Rome were not anywhe re near the port

of Civitavecchia. After an hour and mfteen sinutew

of Dhat lecgan decgared Daw a drive throuGh Lra,ti SandP the giso arrived at 't. keteryw.

lecgan togd hiw dad that the ride fros the port had

sade his feeg giEe he Daw at hose on the S.A. freeDa".

Tver"Dhere "ou gooEed there Daw Gra,ti.

khigip cossentedP b-hereyw proBaBg" a BiGGer underW

cgaww here than the touriwt Bureau Dantw to adsit. Vut getyw not Dorr" aBout that. Ne are here in the Iatican. "othinG here iw defaced. Mt gooEw perfect.é

Nhige the rewt of the HcHurph" sOnaGe wcatteredP

khigip and fasig" entered 't. keteryw Vawigica to the riGht of the YRSx lRRK. A Guide e?pgained that "ou Dougd need the kope if "ou Danted to open the actuag YRSx lRRK itwegf.

Rf courwe jeeGan awEedP bNougdnyt it Be eawier to egecW

trif" it and get peopge Eneeg and pra" in a wpeciag pgaceq -hen the door Dougd !uwt pop open. 'ort of giEe the GateDa" to Yeaven.é

-he Guide waidP bxounG san "ou are BeinG wacrigeGiouw.

-he cuwtos of EeepinG the YRSx lRRK cgowed on agg But the sowt hog" occawionw iw centuriew ogd. "oDP sind "our sannerw and enter Fuietg".é

lecgan pugged hiw Brother throuGh the doorDa" andP

pointinG out acroww Dhat gooEed giEe a vawt sige of peDw and fogdinG chairwP he waidP bLo wit doDn and pra".é

jeeGan did nothinG of the wort. Ye had ween wiGnw atW

tached to the BacEw of chairw agg of the Da" doDn the nave up to the Vernini Agtar. Ye ran to the mrwt one. Mn garGe BgacE print it powtedP b**LIVERPOOL CATHEDRAL 188 m.** é

-

he ne?t wiGn readP **"WINCHESTER CATHEDRAL 170 m.**é

-he ne?t Daw b**ST. ALBAN'S 168 m.**é Cgowewt to the centrag agtar Daw b**WASHINGTON NATIONAL CATHEDRAL 160**

m.é -here Dere no sore wiGnw. jeeGan wpun in circgew Dith hiw arsw out Dide. Ye GraBBed hiw sotheryw hand and decgaredP bM thinE Myve Got itlé

Yiw sotheryw mrwt rewponwe DawP b**SHHHH**111é Vut jeeGan continuedP bHosP thewe wiGnw are the genGthw of the other churchew cospared to thiw one1é keopge pra"inG in the front peDw turned and wiGnaged that Fuiet Daw needed.

Hariegge put her ars around her won and ged his aDa".

Rnce the" Dere out of hearinG diwtanceP jeeGan awEedP bHosP iw that an Mtagian wort of thinGqé

DR. CHARLES S. HANSON58

Hariegge Buwted out gauGhinG and draGGed jeeGan out

around the YRSx lRRK. -he tDo of thes GiGGged untig
khigip and lecgan found thes and awEed Dhat Daw GoinG
on.

-he rewt of the da" Daw a DhirgDind. 'irwt Daw the

'iwtine Chapeg. -he" wta"ed untig the" cougd not gooE up
an" gonGer. "e?t Daw -revi 'ountainU at the interwection
of three Mtagian wtreetw near wose other fasouw Bawigica.
Coinw Dere throDn BacEDard over geft whougderw into the
fountain in hopew of a return trip to Kose

Jjind of giEe wagt at the Eitchen taBgePé waid khigip.
-hen case the 'paniwh 'tepwP the kantheonP the KoW
san 'orusP and the Cogiweus.

jeeGan togd lecgan aBout Ggadiatorw Dho wgiced their

opponentw apart one !oint at a tise wtartinG Dith toew
then feet then mnGerw then handw.

bNe whougd saEe a video Gase out of thatPé proW

cgaised lecgan. bCagg it Lgadiator Sordw of Lore. Neygg Be
richer than rich.é

b7hP M thinE De agread" are richer than rich. Ha"Be De

whougd !uwt tr" to Bu" the CogiweusPé wpecugated jeeGan pugginG a handfug of Turow out of hiw pocEet.

Sate in the da" Dhen the tour Daw mniwhedP the entire

cgan Daw driven BacE to Civitevecchia. At weven p.s. the" agg set in the whipyw sain dininG roos for a feawt Degg dewerved. "one of thes had wtopped for gunch. -he dinner converwation wtarted Dith Dhat the" had ween that

da". Tach tooE turnw and ever"one Daw fawcinated B"
wtoriew untig —asBoree wpoEe up.

bMys diwappointed. M Danted to wee that Uz foot tagg

lavid wcugpture. xou EnoD2the naEed one Dith hiw
hooWhoo uncoveredPé waid —.—. Dith a gawciviouw wsige.

bM thouGht Girgw Dere the onew Dith hooWhoowPé waid
jeeGan.

b"oD jeeGanP Be pogitePé waid hiw dad.
'arah C. contriButedP b-hat wtatue iw not in Kose. Mtyw

in 'gorence. M whougd EnoD. Mys fairg" such of an e?pert
on naEed sen.é

bRh Good Griefl -hiw iw not a converwation for Bo"w or
thewe gittge GirgwPé GroDged jaran.

Tver"one reagi ed that chigdren Dere in the roos. Agg
converwationw wtopped.

-hen Hariegge wpoEe up. bNe Dere in the Yog" Cit"
toda". lid an"one resesBer to pra" for 7ncge Tgonqé

TsBarrawwsent and wh" gooEw ooded the roos
-hen khigip ged a Brief pra"er for the peacefug repowe

of Tgonyw woug and for thanEfugneww for agg that Tgon had
done for hiw fasig". Ye waidP bAHT"Pé and addedP bM thinE
De need to tagE.é

Ye BeGan DithP b-hiw Dhoge wet up iw wtranGe. Ne Go

sowt of our givew pawwinG cawuag converwation and wharinG

ever"da" eventw Dith each other2ordinar" interaction
for ordinar" peopge. "oD De are around each other agg
da" gonGP and De Digg Be for another DeeE. M thinE De
need to whare Dhat De are thinEinG. Ne need to tegg Dhat
De have found out.

DR. CHARLES S. HANSON60

Ye pauwed gonG enouGh for the gittge Eidw to Be corW

ragged at another taBge and Given caEe and ice creas.

Kicardo Dent mrwt. bM as rewearchinG wose of Tgonyw

BacEGround. Howt of "ou EnoD that M DorE independent
contractw for LooGge and

Asa on. M as an invewtiGator. M inwpect iggeGag cgaisw

and attesptw at fraud. Vecauwe of s" DorEP M thinE M
have a wi?th wenwe for riGht and DronG. M as tegginG
"ou that wosethinG iw DronG. Mtyw not Dith our potentiag
inheritance and issinent Deagth. Mt iw Dith the circusW
wtancew wurroundinG 7ncge Tgonyw death. 'irwtP M whougd
tegg "ou that Hariegge and M have Tgonyw sedicag recordw.
Hr. NeatherBourne aggoDed uw to saEe a cop" after De
wiGned an a,davit rewtrictinG uw to privac"P conmdentiagW
it"P and nonWdiwcgowure. -he recordw reveag no heagth
proBgesw. "o heart proBgesw. "o giver diweawe. "orsag
Bgood prewwure and Ggucowe. "o cancer. "othinG1 Tgon
Daw perfectg" norsagg" heagth" Dhen he wuddeng" died.
"o autopw" Daw perforsed Becauwe nothinG untoDard
Daw wuwpected. -he cauwe of death Daw giwted aw JrewpiW
rator" faigure due to ogd aGeWWcgawwic cawe of Jhere toda"
Gone tosorroD.y Mn hiw cawEetP Tgon gooEed giEe he had
wispg" faggen awgeep.é

115

kadricE interruptedP bxewP he weesed to Be dreasinG

Dith a gittge Bit too such saEeup on.é

Kicardo continuedP bTgonyw perfect heagth and wudden

desiwe whougd saEe agg of uw wuwpiciouw. M thinE De need

to reconwider the circuswtancew of Tgonyw death.é

Mn her uwuag wegfWcentered fawhionP —.—. wpoEe up. bM

BeG "our pardonP But he Daw not perfectg" heagth". Ye

cougdnyt Get it up. M sean erectige d"wfunction. Neyre tagEinG that he needed IiaGraP CiagiwP and a BucEet of o"wterw.é

blecganP jeeGanP M wuGGewt that "ou Go viwit the video arcade. -hiw iw a ver" adugt diwcuwwionPé waid Yeather. -he Bo"w Dere eaGer to geave thiw esBarrawwinG soW

sent. jeeGan awEed hiw ogder BrotherP bNhat the hecE iw IianGraqé

-he adugt diwcuwwion continued once the Bo"w Dere Gone.

bM douBt that 7ncge Tgon died fros we?uag d"wfunctionPé

waid khigip. bM sean that he sa" have Danted to die BeW cauwe of wose wort of Sisp Sig" '"ndroseP But it Dougdnyt have Eigged his. Nougd itqé

Yiw Dife rewpondedP bM wuppowe De cougd e?huse Tgon

and checE for wose wort of IiaGra poiwoninG. Aw S.A. Count" Coroner Myve never done that Before. Vut there iw a mrwt tise for ever"thinG.é

bLood ideaPé waid khigip. bYoD san" of "ou thinE the corpwe whougd Be diwinterred and e?asinedqé

Agg handw Dent up.

khigip awEed Yeather to contact her o,ce in the sornW

inG.

bRne sore thinGPé inwiwted Kicardo. b-here iw a GanGW

gand connection in Tgonyw pawt. M diwcovered thiw gawt Dee
E

Before De waiged. M thouGht it Daw isportant to e?pgore
our ancewtr". M contacted Yenr" Souiw Latew MMM. Yeyw
the feggoD on puBgic tegeviwion Dho tracew peopgeyw fasig"
hiwtoriew. Ye togd se he aBwoguteg" cougd not hegp. Ye
and hiw invewtiGatorw ong" gooEed into the BacEGroundw

of fasouw individuagw and actorw. M o ered mve siggion doggarw Dorth of wupport for hiw whoD. -hen he togd se that he cougd hegp. Ye and hiw rewearcherw Dougd taEe on the tawE of tracinG Tgonyw fasig" tree. -hinGw Becase interewtinG DhenP mve da"w gaterP he prewented se Dith a curiouw fact. Tgonyw Grandfather had !oined the Mriwh Vgue Yand 'ociet". M as currentg" rewearchinG thiw Group and Digg get "ou EnoD sore aw M mnd out.é

bNoD1é e?cgaised kadricE Hc'hane. bAn Mriwh sama or wecret wociet"qé

b"ot wurePé waid Kicardo.
kadricE did not hewitate to wa"P bM Dant "ou agg to EnoD

that M EnoD nothinG aBout thiw. Mys MriwhP But M cose fro s

a gonG gine of Mriwh Cathogic kriewtw.é

bM thouGht Mriwh Cathogic priewtw Dere cegiBate. YoD

did "ou Get hereq Naw there a Bawtard conceived in the Begfr"qé awEed 'arah C.

bT"R7LY R' -YA-Pé Boosed jaran defendinG her

huwBand. bNe are not GoinG to diwcuww s" huwBandyw
forefatherw here. Setyw wticE to Tgon and Dhat sa" have
happened to his.é

bM as ong" tr"inG to hegp mGure thinGw outPé inwiwted
'arah C.

bMf there are no sore integgiGent cossentw P getyw cagg it
a niGhtPé waid khigip pointedg".

bRne sore thinGPé waid jaran. b-hat Group that BarGed

in Dith uw at the port in Varcegona. xou EnoD Dho M
seanP the four Dho are wuppowedg" regated to uw Dithin
the diwtant pawt. NeggP M recoGni ed one of thes. -hat
Dosan VeeVee. 'heyw a cop. 'he Gave se a ticEet for

runninG a red giGht three sonthw aGo. "oD whe and her cohortw cgais to Be regated to uw. M donyt Get it. Cop one da". Couwin or wosethinG the ne?tq -hatyw a siGht" BiG coincidence.é

b"o coincidencePé waid khigip.
b'osethinG iw wtinEwPé waid kadricE.
-he Group ad!ourned for the niGht saEinG prosiwew

to mnd out aBout thiw other HcHurph" fourwose. Agg headed to their wuitew gooEinG forDard to an e?curwion to kospeii earg" in the sorninG.
Iia leyCrocicchiP Iia kogiP Iia legge Huratte near VawigW
ica di 'antyAndre 'ratte

CHAPTER 14:

A VISIT TO

POMPEII

When Philip, Hea ther, Declan, and Keegan ar-

rived in Pompeii, they tipped the Limo driver

heavily because the trip from the port at Via Nuova Marina to the Pompeii parking lot was fast (only 20 minutes),
deluxe (what Maserati Ghibli stretch limousine was not),

and the driver, one Guiseppe Verdi Di'Condi, was very entertaining. Guiseppi Arst told them that he had given four well-dressed Tmerican men a ride yesterday. "hey asked him, W?here are the beaches"H Be thought they said, WbitchesH and took them to the Puta Negra Oar in the low life district near the marina.

Philip laughed.

Beather groaned.

Keegan asked, W?hat is a Puta Negra"H

Declan tried to explain that Puta Negra is something

little boys did not need to know about. Ff course the
typical boyhood argument began.

WFh yes they do.H

WFh no they don't.H

WFh yes they do.H

WFh no they don't.H

WFh yes.H

WFh no.H

WFh yes.H

WFh no.H

WFh yes.H

WFh no.H

!inally Philip said, W"hat's enoughjH

"he boys settled down and listened to Guiseppe sing.

WLibiamo, libiamo ne' lieti calici. Let's drink, let's drink

from the Ioyous chalices.H

9n Pompeii, near the rows of souvenir stands and

arched entrance to the scorched city, the family hired a
personal guide who handed them umbrellas. 9t was S0
degrees.

Declan asked 3iri how many degrees Centigrade. Ber

T.9. voice replied, WY2 centigrade. Ouona fortuna.H

Philip commented, W9f the volcano didn't kill the people

of old Pompeii, this heat sure would have.H

"he guide laughed and pointed to Mount Vesuvius

which was looming clear in the distant blue sky. W6es, all

of the people here and in Berculaneum were suzocated

or incinerated.H

WBow far is it from here to Vesuvius"H asked Philip.

WTbout sixteen miles. 6ou could visit it today but there

is a lot to see here in Pompeii. 9t is a choice of seeing

vineyards as you drive up Vesuvius or death, destruction,

and fried bodies here,H answered the guide grinning at

the two boys.

WDeath and destruction,H gloated Keegan raising his

hand for a high Ave with his brother.

WFK, boys. 6ou get your wish,H said Philip. "hen, re-

membering that his kids like gruesome details he added,

WOut remember that only 20,000 people were killed here.

"he Biroshima atom bomb killed ::,000.H

Beather moaned, W"hat's one way to start a tour.H

"he day was miserably hot. "he walk through all of the

city streets was long. Out the tour was a success. "hey

saw the amaEing S0 degree grid layout of the ancient cityU

markets, volcanically preserved bodies, cobbled road-

ways with huge stepping stone crossings, mosaic qoors

under decorated archways, an amphitheater, a grand

plaEa, and private villas with grand rooms, bedrooms,

and private toilet pits.

Oefore stepping into the limo for the return ride to

126

their ship, Keegan had more to say.

 WMom, dad, did you know that this city was not healthy.

3cientists dug the centuries old poop out of the toilet pits
in this place. "hey analyEed it. "hey found out that it was
permeated with Giardia. Giardia means indigestion and
diarrhea were rampant. Pompeii was full of really bad
shitjH

WKRRGTNj "BT"'3 RNFXGBj No more swear words. 9f

you want to continue to be part of this family, you need
to change your language,H said Beather.

Philip lowered his voice to say, W6ou are old enough to
And attention in more positive ways.H

W6es dad,H mumbled Keegan as he pulled his hoodie
over his embarrassed face.

Fnce they climbed into the limousine, Declan whis-

pered to his little brother, WMaybe we should not have
taught you to read.H Be put his arm around Keegan and
gave him a hug.

"hat evening back aboard the big ship the Captain

reJuired all members of the McMurphy group, children
excepted, to meet with him in a private stateroom. ?hen
everyone was present, Captain 'eidenbach introduced
himself again and invited all to be seated. Be cleared his
throat, looked each person in the eyes, and began.

W9'm afraid 9 have some bad news for you. "he body

of your associate, Mr. avier enon, was found qoating
in the waters near 9sola del Gianmutri by Ashermen early this morning. Positive identiAcation was established

through 9nterpol. ?e do not need help identifying his remains. Bowever, we do need help contacting his next of kin. Does one of you have that information"H

 Padrick spoke up. W?e did not know him. ?e were

supposed to meet him onboard. ?e knew that he would be part of our voyage because our uncle's lawyer, Clayton ?eatherbourne, told us so. Fther than that, he was a stranger to us. ?e thought he was an advisor to our

Xncle Rlon. Rither that or he was employed by attorney
?eatherbourne to keep an eye on us. ?e did not know
why he was included in Rlon's will. Be could have been a
government agent for all we know. None of us ever met
him.II

  amboree waved her arms wildly. WNot true. 9 met him

day before yesterday on the lounge deck near the pool.
Be approached me and introduced himself. Be tried to
lure me into one of those private cabanas. 9 believe the
right word is Lothario.' Be even tried to rub suntan oil
onto my shoulders.H

  WRxactly when was this"H asked Captain 'eidenbach.
  W3ometime between when we got on this boat and
before dinner,H answered . .

  "he captain cringed at her reference to WboatH but

chose not to correct her. 3he was Iust another ignorant
Tmerican.

  W3o you met him and then what"H
  W9 noticed him staring at my bikini. 3o 9 covered up

and left. ?e did arrange to meet for Mimosas in the
morning.H

130

WTnd he seemed Iust normally Ane when you left"H JuiEEed 'eidenbach.

W!ine. Maybe better than Ane. 9 think he works out. 9 mean worked outH answered .

Did anyone else meet Mr. avier or know something about him"H

Philip spoke up. W?e did hear the announcements

on the morning of the 'ome excursions. 6ou wanted to know his where abouts. 6ou asked him to report to the

Captain's 3tation. Tfter that we were told that avier evidently had taken a taxi away from the dock much earlier that morning. 9 guess that we should all assume that the person in the taxi was not Mr. enon.H

W9t was not. "he only way Mr. enon's body could have

been found qoating near 9sola del Gianmutri was if he fell overboard in the middle of the night.H

WFr he was pushed,H interIected 3arah C. W9 heard that

scu e in the night and someone went qying. "he scream sounded mannish. 9t wasn't high pitched. Tnd 9 could swear 9 saw a white toupee qoat away on the breeEe. 9 suppose it could have been a small white bird. 3ort of Oye, Oye Oirdie.H

3arah was pleased with her turn of phrase and grinned idiotically.

Karan leaned toward her husband and tried to whis-

per, W3tupid is as stupid saysH modifying !orest Gump's mother's expression.

Captain 'eidenbach didn't brook fools lightly. Be

admonished, WMr. enon deserves more respect than that. 6es, he may have been launched overboard. ?e

are looking into that. Fur security team is reviewing
footage from cameras near the bow, mid-ships, and aft.
"he images are grainy but computer enhancement may
help. ?ith regard to the person who hailed the cab, we
have a lead. "he dockside security cameras recorded
the license plate number. Fne of our security o cers
spoke to the cabbie and found out that the person was a
woman, maybe Ave-foot-two, short blonde hair with blue
eyes. ?e believe she was a passenger. Fnce we track

her down, we'll try to And out if she had any connection
to the disappearance of Mr. enon.H

CHAPTER 15:

ON THE WAY

TO ATHENS

The next day was spent sailing aro und the boot of

Italy and up the Adriatic to Athens. The ship was

so far out to sea that there was not much to see: a few

cruise ships blaring party music, a barge ship container

convoy dotted on top with rows of crows hitching a ride,

and the occasional kshing boat Mying pennants showing the jinds of ksh they had caught.

Rost passengers were spending the day recuperating

from continued Pet lag and from busy days touring Some and Compeii.

Jarah 3. spent the day in her suite ordering room

service and watching reruns of the 3hippendales. Jhe called room to room and told 4amboree to watch channel Nx on the Jhip'etworj. Jhe e'plained that the show was "mantastic" and Kyou"ve never seen se' gods lije this.G

4amboree was otherwise preoccupied. Jhe had picjed

up a kfty something hunj at the bar near the adult pool.
Although he was young enough to be her son, she did
not really care so long as he jept wearing that small blacj
Jpeedo.

Jhortly after noon Chilip called qaran and Rarielle and

suggested that they and their spouses should all meet for
lunch at the -rotto, an e'clusive, zuiet artikcial cave of
a restaurant with blue bacjDlit moss hanging down and
luscious green ferns growing up. Actual Mowing streams
separated tables into small groups surrounded by white
orchids. They would be able to talj privately. The burD
bling streams would mute their conversations.

Rarielle organiVed 1eclan, qeegan, Richi, Reghan,

Raggie, and 4ohnD4ohn into a platoon and marched them
down to the 3hildren"s 5ideo Jzuadroom, a game room
and service provided by the ship so that parents could
drop oB children and have some free time.

The siblings met at the -rotto at U:UE and spent

the ne't several hours eating sushi and discussing their
dilemma. Wecause they started with two rounds of 3ham
3hams the conversation Mowed freely.

Chilip started with, KI have invited that WeeWee woman

to Poin us. qaran is certain that she is the police o?cer
who gave her a red light ticjet bacj home three months
ago. Jhe is the jey to understanding why Lncle Ylon
sent us on this cruise. Jhe should be able to help us
understand Ylon"s passing and the cloaj of mystery surD
rounding his life.G

 KJhe was the one all right,G said qaran loud as usual.

KClease hold it down. Xe need to jeep this conversaD

tion sub rosaU,G said Chilip.

KJubDwhat!G said qaran. The orchids near her vibratD

ed.

KOije in a confessional,G whispered Chilip.

KXe"re confessing!G asjed qaran.

K'ever mind. Oet"s Pust maje sure no one can hear us,G

said Chilip.

They were interrupted by an announcement from the

hostess who had come to their alcove.

KRr. RcRurphy, would you want a lady name WeeWee

and her friends to come to Poin you,G said the hostess

bending near Chilip and cupping her hand near his ear.

The others could hear her. They all answered, KHes.G

Y'tra chairs were brought in and the new group

szueeVed in. There was not zuite enough room at the

table so two sat diagonally at corners bending forward.

Oieutenant WeeWee leaned forward and said, KIt is

time we told you the truth. Xe are all members of the

Oos Angeles police department unit investigating interD

national criminal organiVations. Xe are here undercover

investigating 9avier 9enon. Ry name is Warbara Wrandon Jmith. Yveryone calls me WeeWee. These are my team members Jergeants Oouis Oarue, Oois Sichardson, and Oarry Oambert.G

 KXell2 Hou sure did a great Pob with undercover. I

jnow you. Hou gave me a ticjet for running a red light on Junset Woulevard three months ago,G said qaran dripping with sarcasm and giving WeeWee a hard stare.

DR. CHARLES S. HANSON74

K0h my god. I have a twin sister. That"s her territory.

This is a chance in a million coincidence. It had to be her.
3over blown2 The chances of her giving you a ticjet, and
you thinjing I am her are Pust about nonDe'istent. Wut
that has to be it,G e'plained WeeWee.

KI guess it doesn"t matter now. It made us wonder

about your connection to Lncle Ylon and to this business
with 9avier 9enon,G said qaran.

KI was about to tell you that 9avier 9enon was a memD

ber of an Irish crime syndicate that may be heavy into
drugs, prostitution, and smuggling. $ave you heard of
the Wlue $and Jociety!G asjed Jergeant WeeWee thinjing
that none of this RcRurphy bunch would have even the
faintest jnowledge of the Wlue $and.

Sicardo spoje up.
K'ot only have we heard of the Wlue $and, we have

suspicion that our Lncle Ylon was somehow involved
with it. I researched the Wlue $and this morning and
found out that there is a split in the leadership. 0ne facD
tion wants to continue with involvement in hard drugs.
The other wants to go clean and continue to support
Irish American charities that help new Irish families knd

141

homes and good Pobs. This Jociety has a long history
of doing both. In the UF "s, they smuggled whisjey
and used the money to help illegal Irish immigrant famD
ilies that were pouring into the 3hicago area. Jome of
Wlue $and bosses later demanded repayment. 0thers
forgave debts but wanted loyalty and deeds of support
including turning a blind eye to e'tortion. This Wlue $and
pattern held true until recently. 'ow a faction wants to

turn the Jociety into a E UD3N. A not for prokt charity2 Jo
the current friction is between old world drug lords and
wealthy 'ewDIrish humanitarians.G

 KOast month the Irish Times published a lengthy article

about three lublin knanciers who were murdered. Cost
mortem all three had their arms dyed blue up to the
elbow.G

 K$oly crap2 That"s more information than we have,G
said Oieutenant WeeWee with a looj of astonishment.

 KXhere did you learn all of this!G asjed Jergeant
Oarue.

 KXe are in international waters. Jo I searched the darj

web. It led me to something call the -reen Citch where I
found a good price for stolen Cappy 5an Xinjle N Hear
Seserve at   per bottle,N 3ounty 3orj murder for
hire at UE, , and how to maje a bomb and blame it on
the I.S.A. for . 3raVy stuB, but there was also Wlue
$and Jociety information and a clandestine contact for
"SEEKERS OF THE TRUE BLUE." Xe"ve all zuoted the Wi
ble:
"SEEK AND YE SHALL FIND." I sought and I am alarmed
by what I found. I"m giving you all of the linjs. This one

143

is all yours,G said Sicardo. $e handed his scribbled notes
to Jergeant Oarue.

 Oieutenant Jmith stood up. Jhe rubbed her temples

and waljed toward the ocean view picture window and
bacj. All eyes were on her. Jhe poured a tumbler full of
whisjey from a cut crystal decanter on a side bar. Jhe
lifted it, tipped her head bacj, and swallowed it in one
long gulp.

DR. CHARLES S. HANSON76

K oljs, we have a problem. Ry team is sure that 9avier

9enon was thrown overboard. Xe found threads of pinj
material caught in the davit kttings near where Jarah 3.
witnessed a struggle. On a lower decj balcony we found
his toupee. At least we believe the toupee to be his.
Xe"ll have it analyVed. In short we are certain that 9avier
9enon was murdered. Xe have begun an investigation.
It is lijely that the Wlue $and jilled him or had him jilled.
Xe believe that all of you are in danger. The jiller is still
aboard. If you have any connection to the Wlue $and,
you need to tell us now.G

Chilip raised his hand and was called on.
KI thinj you should start by interviewing 3layton

Xeatherbourne. $e is the one who jnows about 9avier
9enon. $e jnows Rr. 9enon"s a?liation with our LnD
cle Ylon. $e wrote the will that evidently includes Rr.
9enon.G

Oieutenant Jmith reassured Chilip and the whole

group that a talj with Xeatherbourne was her ne't
move. Jhe warned everyone to be cautious and to reD
port any suspicious happenings to her immediately. The
meeting ended with worried loojs from all and an agreeD
ment to meet again late the ne't day.

U Soses are carved into the upper corners of confesD

sionals.

Crohibition years were UF to UFNN.

N 3urrent cost of Cappy 5an Xinjle N is ENFF.FF.

CHAPTER 16:

ATHENS

Keegan had not i magined that he would see most

of the city of Athens from anywhere he stood on the

Acropolis. He stopped near the Erechteion Temple with
its six Caryatids1 and was surrounded by vistas of city
neighborhoods cradled against hillsides beneath distant
mountains as far as the eye could see. He walked toward
the Temple of Athena Nike, and he could see the far
oP city center with its tall buildings. He walked into the

2arthenon and viewed the surrounding megalopolis out beyond the pillars of the temple.I

Dn the 2arthenon he struck a pose and held it. He

imagined he was holding an ancient golden lance with its butt end on the "oor and its spear head pointing skyward.

Weclan came up behind him and tickled his ribs.
'?hatzs up buttercup" Are you frojen in time"- asked Weclan devilishly.

'No, D was Zust imagining D am Athena, powerful godK

dess of war, daughter of Meus,- intoned qeegan in a truly remarkable imitation of Ethel Oerman. He dramatically "ipped the lower portion of his imaginary gown over his shoulder and strode in circles poking the air.

Weclan howled with laughter. A guard warned him to !uiet down. The boys exited the temple.

'Sh my godG Oy little brother thinks hezs a female godK

dess. He could have chosen Meus or Apollo or Atlas, but he chooses Athena. Dzm related to a complete goofball,- shouted Weclan once they were outside.

Heather was close enough to hear him. 'he rushed over and asked if everything was all right.

Weclan explained that 'little brother thinks he is UodK

dess Athena. D think he needs medication and some of that YOANKB2z potion.-

'OANKB2z potion"- asked mom.

'Les, Jud Fight. Dt seems to help dad !uite a bit,- said Weclan with a Ximmy 5allon grin.

'Sh my lord, if you two get any sillier, Dzm going to

need some OANKB2z potion,- said Heather putting her arms through the bent elbows of her darlings and guiding them toward the shade of one of the two trees on the top of the Acropolis.

'Joys, some lady approached you when we got up

here. Lou had run oP to the far side of the Nike Temple so D couldnzt tell who that was,- in!uired Heather.

'That was that nice lady from the ship. Lou know,

blonde hair, blue eyes. D think shezs the wife or girlfriend of that lawyer guy,- said Weclan.

'Ah, Ors. ?eatherbourne. 'o she was Zust being

friendly,- said Heather.

'Les, friendly. Her husband was not with her. There

was one odd thing though. 'he asked us if we had heard

any more about that 0avier 0enon man. D said, YWead is

dead. ?hatzs to hear"z 'he said she was curious then she

Zoined another group and disappeared up the hill,- said

Weclan.

'Thatzs right. They were following and feeding those

stray dogs that live up here. 'trange if you ask me. They

need a dog catcher,- said qeegan. He paused and added,

'Oom, D think she is up here alone because she had an

argument with her husband.-

 Now honey, you shouldnzt try to guess what the lady

is thinking,- said Heather.

'Oom, Dzm not guessing. D saw them arguing in the

atrium of the 8fteenth deck last night after dinner. D

heard her say, 'D want a divorce.-

The family regrouped at the bottom of the AcropoK

lis. qeegan announced that they had climbed down 137

steps. Wid anyone want to race him to the top again"

Sn the return trip to the ship they visited the Ureek

Ouseum where an insistent guide explained that the
entire freeje from the 2arthenon was stolen in 1 I by
Thomas Jruce, the th Earl of Elgin. He grumbled, 'The
beautiful sculptures are in a museum in Fondon, the
bloody Jritish Ouseum. Those damned Jrits need to
return our cultural heritage.-

DR. CHARLES S. HANSON80

1 Sne of these six is in the Jritish Ouseum in Fondon.

Oany people cannot understand why it is not returned
because of its cultural heritage.

1 ?hether or not the 2arthenon was a temple is disK

puted. Dt had no altar. Dt was a treasury at one point.

CHAPTER 17:

MURDER OR

MISHAP

Lieutenant Barba ra Brandon Smit h had been a

homicide detective for the L.A.P.D. for 10 years. She

had helped Detective Hercules Bosch solve a young boy's

murder by proving that clippings from right thumb nails

are much diwerent than those from the left. She had

Oarned the department about J.x.'s gloves and had been

commended for that Oarning after the failed conviction.

SiI months ago she had been promoted to lead detective

for the neO Syndicates and Sociopaths unit. :n the past

the murders she had help solve Oere typical American

type, a bullet to the headK a slashed throatK bodies streOn

across a -eld butchered by an A47TR. She had never even

considered a murder caused by Cipping someone ow the

side of a ship in the middle of the night far from shore.

Ghere Oas no body to eIamine. At least she could not

eIamine it noO. :t Oas in a cryogenic morgue chamber in

komeK the home port of the :talian Moast 'uard ship that
had retrieved the body from the -shermen Oho found
it. Ghe ship she Oas onK this very cruise shipK Oould docF
there in tOo more daysK and she Oould inspect the corpse
at that point. She FneO she Oas fortunate to have a
body at all. zost of these Nover7the7side' bodies Oere
never found. Hungry sharFs and the vagueries of Oind
and Oeather Oere as e"cient as cremation. Ghe bodies
simply disappeared and Oere listed as :.z.E.K :mpossible
to Eind.

 She decided to re7analyVe the scene of the crime. Ghe

ship's railingK the decFK and the nearby Oalls had been
dusted and printed. Ghe railing had a smear of rusty
broOn near the lifeboat Ohere Sarah M. had spent the
night mostly unconscious. Perhaps this Oas blood or
a streaF of darF suntan lotion. Ghe decF Cooring Oas
scrapedK baggedK and readied for a police lab once they
Oere ashore. Ghe davit arm Ohere the pinF -bers Oere
found Oas re7eIamined. Year it Oas a sliver of broFen
-ngernail. Ghat too Oas bagged. :t Oas photographed
before it Oas marFed "59:D5YG:Ak? YA:L zAG5k:AL.X Lo7
cationK timeK and date Oere included.

 Jnce the -ndings at the crime scene Oere eIhaustedK

Lieutenant B.B. Smith and team descended upon the ship's camera and data analytics creO. Ghis Oas a creO **if** you can call tOo people a creO. Jne Oas a computer analyst. Her friends called her PiIel Polly. She could arrangeK scrambleK unscrambleK and otherOise over7an7 alyVe every dot on a computer screen. She specialiVed in improving darFK shroudedK and partial images of human

faces. Ghe other creO member Oas a Nlocations eIpert'
nicFnamed Boing7Boing. Eor some strange reason Bo7
ing7Boing's mind OorFed liFe an echo7locator. 'ive him
a pictureK Ohether blurry or partialK and he could tell
eIactly Ohere that picture had been taFen on the ship.

Lieutenant B.B. asFed PiIel Polly if she had any neO

information about the images from the decF camera on
the night of the scuZe on DecF 1W. Ghe night that some7
one may have been throOn overboard.

"?es sireeKBobKX responded Polly sounding liFe she

came out of the 1j00's in the rural south. ":n fact these
images turned out pretty good once : coloriVed them.X

"MoloriVedqX asFed Sergeant B.B.

"?esK the original images Oere dull gray and light blacF

so : sorted the piIels. Some piIels revealed actual origi7
nal color. Ghe rest : had to guess at.X

Polly turned the computer screen toOard the lieu7

tenant. Ghere Oas a clear image of an older man easily
recogniVed as —avier —enon and a youngerK much short7
erK Ooman Ohom she identi-ed as passenger ee ee
eatherbourne.

"Do you Oant to see Ohat happened neItqX asFed

Polly.

"?es sireeK BobKX teased B.B.

Ghe recording shoOed that ee ee abbed —avier full

force in the necF. She had seen that move on a Blue

Bloods rerun the night before in her room.

—avier —enon choFed but found the strength to catch

ee ee's arm and lift her above his head. He balanced

her liFe a log. He stepped up tOo rungs on the ship's

railing. ith the NAtlas7zove' from the orld restling EederationK he shrugged and pushed up and out in a motion that Oould send ee ee hurtling over the side.

  ee ee desperately reached doOn and caught the

railing Oith her left hand and she hooFed her right hand through his belt. —avier teetered. ee ee clung tight and pulled doOn Oith all of her strength. —avier tippedK CailedK and CeO out over the side liFe a spastic bird sOat7 ting at air that could not lift him.

  ee ee pulled herself up the outside of the railingK

managed to Cip one leg over the top rungK and fell side7 long to the decF.

  5veryone Oatching the video Oas stunned and silent. Ghen Sergeant Larue saidK " ellK that solves that. Yot zurder. zore liFe fortunateK aOFOard self7defense.X "?esK evidently these tOo had some sort of hatred that is hard to imagineKX said Sergeant Lambert.

"YJG HAkDKX said Pilel Polly. "5ach camera is

e uipped Oith audio. Gheir last Oords are recorded. : imagine you'd liFe to hear that.X "kight noOKX said Lieutenant B.B.

Polly turned up the volume and everyone heardK "?ou

bitch. hat gives you the rightqX yelled by —avier.

": videoed you in bed Oith my husband. Ghat gives me

the right. ?ou have ruined my marriage.X

"?ou god aOful bitch. He doesn't need your interfer7

ence anymore.X

"?ou saO Ohat happens neIt. He picFs her up and tries

to throO her overboardKX said PiIel Polly.

5veryone sat doOn puVVledK disgruntledK and Oonder7

ing Ohat to do neIt.

":'m sorry PollyK but Oe need to discuss this privately.

Ghis is noO a ma or crimes investigation. ?ou must Feep

this tape and all of its information to yourself. : mean

both you and your partner over there zr. Boing.X

 "He's 'us. He Oon't say a Oord.X

 Sergeant Lois kichardsonK Oho had been uiet up to

this pointK interrupted. "'usK can you identify the loca7

tion of this pictureqX She pointed to an image on her

i7phone that shoOed the bacFs of —avier —enon and Mlay7

ton eatherbourne outside a ship's door.

 "?esK of courseK that is the door to the ship's private

collection of ancient manuscripts. ?ou'll -nd it in the rare

booFs sectionKX ansOered 'us in the matter of fact voice

of someone Oho FnoOs it all.

 Polly and 'us left the room.

" e have choicesKX said BeeBee. ": do not thinF Oe

should arrest zrs. eatherbourne.   e shouldn't divulge

Ohat Oe FnoO. :f Oe did and all of this Oent publicK

all of our leads Oould go dead. Jn the other handK Oe

noO FnoO that —avier —enon Oas intimate Oith Mlayton

eatherbourne. e need to -nd out if eatherbourne

Oas part of this Blue Hand Society.

Ghat evening after the ship set sail for 9eniceK Lieu7

tenant Smith and her three Sergeants met in the ice

163

cream parlor Oith the entire zczurphy gang including
all of the children and both of 5lon's eI7Oives.

Sarah M. complained that she preferred gelato. xam7

boree saidK ": Oant a tall glass of zAY goK er man7
go get itqX

4aran groaned. Her husband stucF his -nger in his
mouth and pretended to puFe.

hen 4eegan saO kicardo's faFe puFeK he had to do

the same. He faFe barfed around the table then stood
on a chair and pretended to -ll a trash can Oith vomit.

All laughed.

Ghen the lieutenant told everyone that she had no
neO neOs. "—avier —enon is in the morgue in kome. Ghe
eatherbournes are dining in their rooms. Maptain kei7

denbach says all is Oell. zy team and : Oill continue to
investigate the Blue Hand.

CHAPTER 18:

THE CANALS

OF VENICE

The McMurphy s hip and nine othe rs arrived at the

harbor in Venice at the same time. The port had only

six dedicated passenger terminals. So three ships had to
tender their passengers to various Venetian piers.

 The McMurphy's had the good fortune of docking at

the main terminal at the northwestern end of the city. A quick cab ride brought them near enough to the Grand Canal that they could walk their rolling luggage to their hotel.

Because they would spend the night at the Hotel

Danieli1 they knew that they had no right to complain about prices. But a can of Coke at $10 and a Peach Bellini at $55 brought groans of "Death to Il Duce." The drink bill for the family was $490 plus tip.

Keegan saw the total and told his dad that he could buy a new PlayStation for that much.

The whole family went to St. Mark's Basilica after

dinner for Vespers. Declan imagined that everyone was praying for better prices. Keegan imagined that the entire city would sink under the weight of price gouging, but he kept it to himself.

Drinks, dinner, prayers meant that it was time for

some fun. They all walked through a rabbit warren of streets and were guided by some locals to Gelato Veniticio Superbo.

Everything was great until Mr. and Mrs. Weather-

bourne showed up. She was crying. He was smoking a cigar.

Keegan leaned toward his brother and whispered, "Damned pigeons!"

"Little boys aren't supposed to cuss," said Declan. "Those birds have crapped on ZeeZee's black Battenburg collar. That's why she is crying," said Keegan.

"I'm gonna crap on you if you keep cussing. What in the damned hell is Battenburg?" said Declan.

"It's lace. Battenburg black with pigeon shit on it," said Keegan.

That was the signal. Declan grabbed Keegan under

the arm pits and tickled. "You are a very bad little boy,"
he growled in Keegan's ear.

The group greeted the Weatherbourne couple.

Padrick asked Clayton if he would please smoke outside.
In an egotistical huR, Clayton strode past him not saying
a word.

Heather took ZeeZee by the hand and guided her

away from the gelato courtyard before anyone could ask

her why she was so upset. They found a bench near
the Doge's Palace. Although the area was busy with the
overjow from the nine huge tour ships, no one paid
attention to pretty friends chatting.

"What has happened?" asked Heather.

"I'm getting a divorce," said ZeeZee.

"Xight here in the middle of Venice?" asked Heather
with a light hearted smile.

ZeeZee caught on and said, "It would serve him right.

Maybe I should throw a party and throw him into the
canal, one of the back canals with all of the slop and
garbage in it."

Immediately after saying that her mind proOected

throwing …avier oR the side of the ship into the midnight
sky. She covered her face. That was when she noticed
the blob of bird poop on her collar.

"zh my dear god. Do you have anything to wipe oR
this mess?" asked ZeeZee.

Heather reached into her purse, found Handi-Wipes,
and gave one to ZeeZee.

"This is how my day has gone. I am the target for

pigeon shit."

Both women laughed.

"Divorce is a drastic step. Who is she"" asked Heather.

"That's the problem. He is having an aRair with a

man," said ZeeZee knowing that the aRair had come to
a sudden end.

"A man? Who on earth wouldUU."

"...avier ...enon," blurted ZeeZee.

"The dead man?"

"StiR!" said ZeeZee who burst out in uncontrollable
laughter when she realiNed what she had Oust implied.
It took more than a minute for the ladies to bring their
morbid sense of humor under control.

"That bastard is actually why I am here. I wanted to

:nd you and give you this. I think it incriminates him. I
think he is, let's say was, part of a criminal organiNation.
That's bad enough, but it would be even better if this
came back and bit Clayton too."

ZeeZee handed Heather a large thin portfolio en-

velope and said, "I've read the contents. I know your
husband is a lawyer. He will know what to do with this."
ZeeZee's face was lined and worried, but a thin smile was
lit by the Venetian sunset.

Heather reached into the envelope. The wax seal had

already been broken. When held back together the two
pieces formed a hand, a blue hand designed to clasp
the portfolio closed. Whereas most o2cial seals were
imprinted on ruby red wax, this was not. The wax was
royal blue. Heather withdrew a single sheet of blue
parchment. zn it was a re:ned drawing of a right hand
with its index :nger pointing at gold leaf lettering. The

171

oversiNed lettering spelled out the name of …avier …enon. 3nder the name was inscribed GXAíD MASTEX. Below that was printed a codeF A1-Z-éèPP Zurich. In addition each corner of the page displayed an ultramarine hand-print. 3nder each print was the slogan, "ALL zX íziE." The upper half of the page was embossed with an eagle gripping a golden scepter in its talons. zn the scepter were inscribed the words "Contae Corca) ag 6inbar's."é

The lower half of the page was similarly decorated except that in the talons of the lower eagle was a sword. The sword bore the Gaelic words, "Ar Chladach ía Sicile is Lapis LaNuli an Doras."è

"It looks like Mr. ...enon was high up in this organiNa-

tion. A grand poobah or something. I smell danger. If he was the leader and he had an account in Zurich, we are in trouble," said Heather. "I think we take this to my husband right now. I think he will want those L.A. cops involved."

"ío! They will tell Clayton. Clayton cannot know that I

am involved in this," said ZeeZee. She knew her husband would go craNy because of the theft of this document. She also carried the guilt of having seen ...avier ...enon fall into his wet grave.

"ZeeZee, you have my room phone number and here

is my cell number. Call me if you need my help. Better than that, call me if you need my friendship. I will share this with my husband as soon as I :nd him. He will be amaNed and disturbed that ...avier ...enon could ever have been included in our uncle's will. Surely the cryptic code will lead to ...avier's murderer."

"Surely," said ZeeZee afraid to reveal anything about her part in …avier's death.

Heather knew how important this blue document was.

She hid it under the bodice of her blouse and set out to :nd her husband and boys. She assumed that they might still be eating gelato at Gelato Veniticio Superbo in the Cannaregio neighborhood. The trouble was that the sections or neighborhoods or areas of Venice all ran together. She took a right, two lefts, and went straight over the a bridge. ío Gelato Superbo. So she went back over the bridge and took a left, a right, and another left. More canals. More bridges. Hundreds of shops. She decided to try her cell phone. To her surprise Mapquest worked :ne, only it was in Italian. She thumbed in "Dove diavolo il Gelato Superbo?"4 zf course it was around the next corner. zut front, there they were one with chocolate, one mango, one coconut.

Philip signaled for her to Ooin them.
""Can't right now," she said. She tapped her blouse

and tried to show the edge of the envelope she had hidden.

Her husband had seen her make any number of signs

that it was time for romance, but this was a new one. He stood up, walked over and put his arms around her, kissed her on the neck and asked if things were all right.

She pulled the hidden envelope out and said, "You won't believe this."

The family retreated to their suite of luxury rooms.

An hour later and ten websites deep, Philip and Heather had discovered only two factsF 1 the address of a bank in SwitNerland and é veri:cation that the CzDE A1-Z-éèPP was for billionaires and pharmaceutical companies.

 Before they went to dinner with their boys, Philip

contacted Lieutenant Smith and handed over the incrim-inating blue evidence to her.

TRUE INHERITANCE 93

is $ 1 9 including taxes and fees.

é County Cork at 6inbar's

è zn Sicily shores Lapis LaNuli is the door.

4 Where in the hell is Gelato Superbo?

CHAPTER 19:

MT. ETNA

AND A DOOR

TO VIOLENCE

The clan disemba rked at Messina Harbor, Sicily at

8 a.m. The early start was needed because Mt. Etna

was usually clear in the morning but haloed by clouds from midday on. Some wanted to travel up the volcano and enjoy the spectacular view. Others wanted to go their separate ways and see the sights of the island. None wanted to spend another entire day together. They hired private guides with limousines, and oP they went.

Khilip, Deegan, "eclan, and Marielle

 ?"ad, this is an active volcano, right"k asYed Deegan as the limo neared the highest point of the drive.

?Ies, son. 't is the most active volcano in Europe. 'n

fact youWll see the steam and bubbling lava vent today.k

 ?xell, dad, what ' donWt understand is that this thing

has e-ploded year after year yet people Yeep right on

building.k

 ?Deegan, you have to remember that the seismic acC

tivity is monitored. So at least we Ynow we are safe for

today.k

 ?"ad, once we risY death at the top, is there any

chance we could go to the 1ity of 0BB Jells"k

 ?' guess we could. xhy" xhatWs there"k

 ?'t has the 1hocolate Museum. ThatWs probably the

best place on the island,k said Deegan licYing his lips.

 "eclan chimed in, ?Maybe we should go to the 1hocoC

late Museum Rrst before it melts oP the side of the

mountain.k

 ?My vote is fumaroles then chocolate rolls,k said

Heather.

Sarah 1. and Famboree F.

 Sarah 1. and Famboree F. decided to team up. They

rented a Golls Goyce and a young body builder guide.
They gave speciRc instructions.

?Airst, we want to go to the VreeY zmphitheater at

Taormina. ' want to sing zve Maria and hear how it
sounds,k said Sarah 1ambionetta.

?' will give you a thousand dollars not to sing,k sugC
gested Famboree Fane. ?' thinY we should go to the nude

beach and then to Messina MagniRca, the jewelry store
at qia 1anniòòaro where the rich and famous shop.k

They decided that all three places were possible and

asYed the guide to taYe them Rrst to a store to buy towels
so that they could dry oP after a dip at the nude beach.

The guide said, ?'n Sicilia lasciamo asciugare lWacùua

sulla nostra pelle. Kué essere leccato via pií tardi. Eh,
thatWs eh, OnCeh Sicily we letCeh the salt water dry onCeh
our sYin. 't canCeh be licY!d oPCeh later.k

The ladies both said, ?SL, sL, molto bene:k

Marielle, Gicardo, Maggie, Meghan, Michi, and

FohnCFohn

The leather seats of the Maserati Vhibli limousine with

Marielle, Gicardo, Maggie, Michi, and little Satan were
smeared with the gelato they had bought at a driveCthru.
They were on their way to Kasta Karadiso near the old
town of Taormina. This place was for children. The family
voyage had been too serious for too long. Kasta Karadiso
was the 'talian version of (ego (and. Everything was
made out of pasta, plastic pasta that is) Gigatoni, Jow
Tie Aarfalle, Spaghetti, "italini, Jucatini, zngel Hair. Iou
name it. They had it. Ged, green, yellow, blue, pinY,

182

orange, purple, white, blacY, and indigo. There were castles, bridges, towers èincluding a leaning replica of the tower in KisaX. There were trains, airplanes, cars, and trucYs. Kasta òoo animals roamed between e-hibits. Jecause some of the pasta broYe oP at times, there were signs everywhere that said, ?NO EzT. NO Sxz(C

(Ox. 1HODE. 1HODE. "Ez": "Ez": MOGTO 4 MOGTO:k Jecause the plastic pasta was durable, Yids could sit on it, YicY it, tumble it, and stand it up again. There were even pasta games) 1ornCHoleCtheCKasta, Kin the Tail of the Kasta, Splat the Kasta Sauce, and Swim the "ry Kool of Soft Elbow Kasta.

The Yids had a blast and then even more fun hapC

pened. There were pasta eating contests. Iou picY the pasta. Iou picY the marinara. Iou weigh it. Iou eat it. zll with a timer of course. Kriòes were given for fastest, most, and sloppiest. xhat a mess: znd what fun: FohnCFohnWs sYy blue boyWs shirt and shorts turned spaghetti sauce red.

Gicardo and Marielle laughed until they cried. They

were so distracted by Kasta Karadiso that they barely heard what they were sure were RrecracYers in the disC tance.

Daran and KadricY

Daran and KadricY were fascinated by the VreeY temC

ples on the island. There were more VreeY ruins on Sicily than in any other place in the Mediterranean. There was the "oric Temple at Segesta, the Temple of Funo at zrigento, the Temple of 1oncordia, the zrigento "ioscuri with only four "oric columns still standing, and the masC sive Temple 1. Selinus. The list went on but they could not visit them all because sites were strung out across the island.

Their attention did not stray bacY to Elon McMurphy,

1layton xeatherbourne, or 7avier 7enon for even a moC ment. They were truly amaòed to see so many interesting temples that had been built before the 1hristian Era.

The drive bacY to the ship was lovely with vistas

stretching out across the blue Mediterranean lit by the late afternoon sun. xhen they reached Messina, they heard round after round of RreworYs in the distance. They wondered what holiday it was and who was celeC brating.

The (ieutenant and Sergeants

(ieutenant Jarbara Jrandon Smith, Sergeant (ouis

(arue, Sergeant (ois Gichardson, and Sergeant (arry (ambert had met early that morning with the Sicilian Kolice "epartment 1hief of 1osa Nostra 'nvestigations. They shared the blue parchment document with 7avier 7enonWs name on it with the 1hief, a man named 1apone de 1oraòone, of all things. The chief saw the (apis (aòuli imprimatur and Ynew immediately that he now had the evidence he needed to arrest all of the members of the Messina 1osa Nostra. They had murdered the infamous maRoso zlfonso de 1orelione de Kacino. They had comC mitted this Yilling in an ePort to capture the very blue parchment document now in police possession. The legal deed that had the Jlue Hand banY name and code on it.

 The chief e-plained that (apis (aòuli, when crushed to a Rne powder, was a pure deep blue, and this powder

was turned into the inY for tattoos on the arms and hands
of the Sicilian branch of the Jlue Hand Society, the bitter
enemies of the 'rish Jlue Hand.

 Even though it was illegal, 1hief 1oraòone armed the

(.z. detectives with zD U s and grenades. He brought his
sùuad of sharp shooters together and announced, ?xe
do this now:k

 The 1hiefWs police and the (.z. team loaded into unC

marYed vans and headed to MessinaWs famous qiale JocC
cetta. 't was Ynown as the Street of Jlood because of the
many gangland Yillings that had happened there over the
years.

 ?xe will go to the (apis (aòuli Aoundation and arrest

these Yillers,k bragged the chief with his chest puPed out
and his cigar pinched tightly in the corner of his mouth.
?'taly will have its revenge:k

 The street was ùuiet. The chief YnocYed on the (apis

SocietyWs carved oaY door with the butt of his gun. The
door swung open. The chief announced, ?xe bring news
from 7avier 7enon.k Those were the last words he ever
spoYe. The òi gun Rre was immediate and devastating.
The chief and three of his subordinates caught bullets in

188

the face and necY. They were dead before they hit the
ground. (ieutenant Smith ducYed, rolled, and came up
Rring. z bullet had whiòòed through her hair, graòed her
scalp, and landed in the chest of Sergeant (arue. He died
with his eyes wide open in surprise. (ieutenant SmithWs
bullets hit two capos who spun in midair, cursed Vod and
died on the doorstep. znother round of machine gun
Rre burst through the doorway. Sergeant Gichardson

was shot in the left shoulder and fell to the ground.
xith her right hand she unfastened a Morpheus Alash
Jlast grenade from her belt and pitched it through the
(apis (aòuli doorway. The e-plosion was deafening. The
ash was blinding. Then there was silence, ear piercing

silence, just before the roof of the building collapsed and
buried all within.

Khilip, Heather, "eclan, and Deegan

Khilip, Heather, "eclan, and Deegan saw the e-ploC

sion. They were driving bacY from the long dayWs journey
up Mt. Etna and over to the 1ity of 0BB Jells. They had
seen the 1hocolate Museum, the only airCconditioned
building in town. They had eaten their Rll of chocolate
tru es. zs they neared the Street of Jlood, the limouC
sine driver slammed on the braYes and threw the vehicle
into reverse. He bacYed through streets at top speed.
Stray dogs and alley cats scattered. The bacY of the limo
smashed into the mooring stanchion nearest the gang
planY to the cruise ship. The driver yelled, ?Vet out. Gun
for your lives.k

Sirens were sounding throughout the city. zll roadC

ways were blocYed by police and local maRa guards. Kolice were summoned from all surrounding cities. Jy 0B p.m. the city was under curfew.

zll passengers, including the (.z. detectives, were

loaded onto the ship. The body bag with Sergeant (arueWs remains was hauled over shoulder up the ramp. Sergeant Gichardson was brought on board in a stretchC er. z bloodied (ieutenant J.J. Smith was bandaged by the shipWs doctor. Sergeant (ambert, who had been wounded in a leg, limped onboard. znchor was weighed. The ship departed in record time with full permission of the Harbor Master. The whole damned mess would have to be sorted out in the morning.

CHAPTER 20:

A VISIT FROM

THE MEDIA

By noon the next day the ship was safely docked at

Civitavecchia. The cruise line terminal had truly earned
its name: CELEBRITY CRUISE LINES. The harbor was
overrun with media. Cameras, news crews, CNN, Eu-
ronews, Antichità Chiossone, and MSNBC were all present in one form or another. NBC's Lester Holt and ABC's
David Muir were allowed on the ship because so many
of the passengers were American. Both Holt and Muir
were amazed and disgusted because they had read local
tabloid headlines declaring:

SHIP ATTACKED BY COSA NOSTRA

PASSENGERS GUNNED DOWN ON THE HIGH SEAS

SICILIAN MURDERERS AVENGE THE DEATH OF BENIT
O

MUSSOLINI

Nothing but obvious, misleading nonsense. All of this

needed to be straightened out and reported truthfully
and accurately.

When they met with Captain Reidenbach, the port

o"cials, and an Interpol investigator, David Muir cut to
the chase.

?Was this incident connected to the Elon McMurphy

passengers"j

The captain answered, ?No it was not. A unit from

the Los Angeles division of Syndicates and Sociopaths
was on our ship. They were undercover investigating
Cosa Nostra connections. They went ashore in Messina and shared information with the chief of the police agency assigned to Maqa dealings, a man named
Captain Capone de Corazone. Captain Corazone and his
agents xoined with the Los Angeles police investigators
and paid a visit to one of the local maqa headXuarters.
The maqosos opened their door and come out shooting.
Captain Corazone and three of his men were killed in

the qrst volley. So was one of the L.A. detectives, a man named Sergeant Louis Larue. Three other L.A. police o"- cers were wounded. They are all e'pected to fully recover. One of those o"cers saved the day. Though gravely wounded, she managed to lob a Morpheus Grenade into the building in the middle of heavy gunqre. The building collapsed. That's about it.j

?There is a report that one of your passengers fell

overboard and drowned seven days ago, early in your
itinerary. That man was avier enon. Was he connected to the incident yesterday in Messina harbor"j asked
David Muir smoothing his brilliantined hair.

?This is an ongoing investigation,j stated the man from

Interpol. ?I can tell you that we are looking into his
connection or possible association with the Sicilian Cosa
Nostra, but that is o the record.j

Lester Holt asked, ?Are any of the misleading headlines in the local news true"j

The Captain answered, ?No. In fact we received a

call from Rupert Murdoch himself assuring us that he
controls the tabloids in this part of the world. He said
that the headlines are xust sensationalism designed to
sell newspapers.'j

Lester scratched his head. He knew that news report-
ing and factual reality are two di erent things.

The brieqng ended with a pointed reXuest from the
Captain.

?Please report no names until we can verify that the
ne't of kin have been notiqed.j

196

Lester Holt and David Muir reported the facts of the

incident on their nightly news programs. They included
visuals of the collapsed Lapis Lazuli headXuarters and
photos of blood on the street in Messina.

CHAPTER 21:

PREPARATION

FOR

ANOTHER

VISIT TO

ROME

Celebrity Cruise Lines allowed pas sengers to stay

onboard for one more night in safe harbor, if they

chose to do so. Most departed battling media and the paparazzi blitz until they disappeared on the highway and into the vastness of Rome.

The McMurphy group stayed. They met for dinner in the ship's BEEF AND SEA RESTAURANT. Their children were cared for by the ship's child care and parent relief staP.

"hilip began the dinner discussion.
xTomorrow will be an eWciting day. He meet in the

private conference room at the Baglioni de Bernini Cotel not far from the "hurch of the Coly Mother of "hrist. He may want to pray before and after,G he said with humor and sarcasm.

Ce continued, xUncle Elon's will will !nally be read.

After that, we face real challenges. The sheer amount of our inheritance has attracted international attention, and the gun!ght yesterday has somehow landed in our laps. Media pundits are hinting that we are connected to and responsible for eliminating the Messina branch of the Sicilian "osa Nostra. kood griefY He had nothing to do with those Xillings. Ies, we Xnow that Uncle Elon Xnew about the Blue Cand. Some of us also suspect that Lavier Lenon was somehow connected to the incident yesterday. The day before yesterday my wife was given a document that shows that Lavier Lenon was a member of the Blue Cand Society. That document indicates that Mr. Lenon was probably high up in the organization. ?t also lists a banX in Switzerland and a code which is most

liXely a banX account linX. The document is embossed
with Blue Cand "ounty "orX information and with Sicilian
-apis -azuli particulars. Iesterday's gun battle was at the
-apis -azuli address. My wife and ? want you to Xnow that
we gave the document to -ieutenant Smith on the day
before yesterday. That's all we Xnow. Then the gun!ght.
The two must be connected.G

Ricardo's brow furrowed. Ce put both elbows on the

dinner table and leaned forward. Ce said, xIes they are connected. Blue Cand and -apis -azuli are two arms of the same body. ? researched the darX web even farther. The site draws a circle around them both. They may be interlinXed or opposing groups of the same mob. Hho Xnows He are only involved because we are inheriting money from someone who was somehow associated with these factions. "erhaps we will !nd out more to morrow.G

Ricardo raised his elbows, leaned his chair bacX on two legs and began rocXing.

xSpeaXing of tomorrow,G said "adricX McShane reach

ing out to maXe sure that Ricardo did not tip over. x? have arranged for a helicopter to y us to the Bernini Cotel. They have a heliport on the roof. That way we will not have to deal with media or be hounded by paparazzi.G

CHAPTER 22: THE READING OF ELON MCMURPHY'S WILL

All members of t he McMurphy ass emblage met

at 10 a.m. in the Palazzo Conference Room of

the Bernini Grand. The room was more suited for the
courtiers of Louis XIV that for a gathering of Southern
California casuals in sandals and short sleeved summer
outyts.

ClaWton B. -eatherbourne began the meeting bW saW,

ing" Hpello friends" we are gathered to hear the ynal wishes of our comEanion Mlon "c"urEhW.?

PhiliE thought" HComEanionk -hat the hellk pas ClaW, ton forgotten who he is talNing tok?

peather asNed" H-ill Wour wife be with us todaWk? -eatherbourne cleared his throat" straightened his

tie" and stated that she would not. She had caught an earlW Jight home

pe continued the meeting bW stating" HMlon was in

everW waW a good Eerson. pe was reserved and intro, verted. But good to the core. pe invested wiselW and amassed a fortune. jow it is time for Wou to Nnow the Earameters of Wour inheritance. PerhaEs Wou thinN that I will read from a legal EaEer todaW. I will not.?

ImmediatelW Oamboree sEoNe uE" HI thought we are

here for the reading of the will.? She adUusted her Gucci fedora so that it tilted slightlW to the right.

Hjo. jo reading. Instead Wou will hear from Mlon "c, "urEhW himself with a Ere,recorded video.?

ClaWton yddled with the comEuter on the table in front

of him. Fn a huge comEuter screen on the oEEosite wall aEEeared 'ncle Mlon" bright as daWlight" clear as summer sun.

The recording began.

Hpello everWone. The fact that Wou are gathered here

listening to this means that I am no longer EhWsicallW with Wou. I do hoEe that in some sense I am with Wou in memorW and in sEirit.?

DR. CHARLES S. HANSON110

Hqirst" I would liNe to aEologize. I have not been the

best uncle" friend" advisor" or conydant. I:ve alwaWs been
one to lead a Auiet life tucNed awaW in mW own little corner
of the world. I hoEe that mW will" mW true wishes will
mend mW short comings and bring us together.?

HponestlW" I thought I would live for several more Wears

and that I would be able to gift Wou the moneW I have
accumulated in Eerson. The fact that I am not standing
here means that something went wrong.?

HI do not mean to uEset Wou" but I must tell Wou

that three Wears ago I began to susEect that I might be
Eoisoned or murdered. I was in mW basement tossing
out old EaEers and faded Eicturcs whcn I camc across
something Auite curiousY a Eicture of mW grandfather on
mW father:s side. In it he wore a blue silN gown and a
sEiNe toEEed hat. The Eicture was attached to a blue
Earchment document that was embossed with a yne
reElica of an eagle holding a Eennant in its talons. Fn
the Eennant was grandEa:s nameY qIjB'R "C"'RPp8.
Below that were the words 9CountW CorN" qull,Jedged
"ember of The Blue pand SocietW: and the date Fctober
13" 16DK.?

HI was more than a little surErised to ynd out that

207

mW grandfather had Uoined a secret societW. I wanted to

Nnow more. qirst ox" I wanted to ynd out if qinbar and

I were related to this grouE in CountW CorN" Ireland. I

submitted mW j' and found out that it was true. -ith

no chance for statistical error" I am descended from a

familW of fabric dWers in the town of nocNnagree" CountW

CorN.?

Hje t thing I wanted more information about the Blue

pand SocietW. -as it a charitWk -as it a cabalk id it

sEring from the Catholic Churchk -as it an underworld

organizationk I tried to ynd out" but this was a trulW

secret societW. I discovered that the onlW waW to obtain

the Nnowledge I wanted was to Uoin uE. I had to submit

j' Eroof that I am CountW CorN Irish. I had to be related

to a Nnown Blue pand member. That was easW. I had

qinbar:s membershiE Earchment and his birth certiycate.

I also had to write out a checN for two million dollars. That

was even easier.?

HI was admitted to the clandestine world of the Irish

Blue pand SocietW. Mncoded websites were given to me.

The SocietW oEened its secrets to me. I attended Erivate

meetings and found out that all was not well within the

Blue pand leadershiE. The leaders had sElit into two

factions.?

HFn one side was a humanitarian faction who Auoted

the original EurEose of the societW. It was to suEEort

immigration to 'merica bW imEoverished Irish families

who could no longer suEEort themselves in Ireland be,

cause the dWes for the fabric businesses theW owned had

sNWrocNeted in cost. TheW were going out of business.
TheW were starving. The Blue pand SocietW Erovided a
waW out" no more hunger" and a solid Uob with a stable
future. Immigrants reEaid the SocietW as theW became
established" grew richer" and banded together in ever
greater numbers to suEEort the cause.?

 HThen the sElit came. ' greedW faction in CorN was
oxered a fortune to sell street drugsY mariUuana" co,

caine" heroin" methamEhetamine" and an absolute ton of
o WmorEhonecodone" also Nnown as o W,". 'n Italian
mob from SicilW was involved. The drugs were manu,
factured bW and imEorted from several Sicilian towns.
TheW were shiEEed directlW to CountW CorN in vintage "r.
Mtna wine barrels. The Sicilians had no trouble corruEting
the 'merican and MuroEean Eharmaceutical comEanies
who were Eromoting o WmorEhonecodone. PrescriE,
tions were written in Sicilian cities. Then theW were ylled
bW direct mail to the island. PeoEle throughout ItalW and
MuroEe became addicted to these drugs.?

HThe Blue pand SocietW faction wanted minimum in,

volvement. These Irish were willing to trW the drug a little
if it meant a lot of moneW to suEEort Irish immigrants in
Chicago and jew 8orN. This faction soon found out that
o W," meant Eure addiction for Irish or anW other na,
tionalitW. It was a non,discriminant Niller. The onlW thing
that could be done was to bacN awaW from all dealings
with the Sicilians.

The Sicilian Cosa jostra had become addicted to the

moneW and the drugsY a malignant combination. These
mobsters formed the Sicilian LaEis Lazuli SocietW.

 HI decided to trW to do something about this horror.

I found an agent and allW within the Blue pand" a man named Xavier Xenon" whom bW now Wou have met. "r. Xenon and I reorganized the Irish Blue pand. -e formed a grouE of wealthW 'merican and Irish" both men and women. -e tried to breaN awaW from the drug Eeddlers. -e created a not,for,Eroyt corEoration and tooN over the SocietW:s ynances.?

Hjow" Wou must be wondering. -hat does all of this

have to do with mW 'ncle Mlon:s wishesk pow could such

an introvert have done anW of thisk -hW did Mlon want

to send us on a MuroEean voWagek The answers are

straight forward. qirst" bW shiEEing Wou out together

as one grouE" I thought Wou would discover a common

goal bW meeting Xavier Xenon. I assume that Wou have

met him and that Wou have a solid Elan to imErove the

chances of a Eositive future for the Blue pand SocietW.

It will be a chance to do some real good in the world.

PerhaEs Wou will do what I could not. Second" Wou are

familW. 8ou must do what I could not do. 8ou must

learn to directlW suEEort each other. 8ou need to live

interconnected lives. "W wish is that Wou should do what

I did not. Please" Elease connect the dots and sEend the

rest of Wour lives helEing EeoEle who are less fortunate

than Wou. Third" Wou will inherit e Eansive amounts of

moneW" but that cannot be Wour true inheritance. Riches

can be the cause of great Eersonal harm. Riches can also

be Eersonal salvation if Wou will onlW choose the righteous

Eath.?

HBut that is enough sermonizing. 8ou will do what Wou

want. I wish Wou well.?

HI do have one ynal reAuest.   I maW have died an

213

untimelW death. Please e Elore how I died. Please right
anW wrongs.?

 H"W 'ttorneW" ClaWton -eatherbourne will now give

Wou legal documents that divide mW holding amongst
Wou. I do want the best for Wou. I would do more if I
could.?

DR. CHARLES S. HANSON114

The video ended.   jo 9I love Wou.:   jo 9Peace and

qarewell.: FnlW the heartfelt earnestness of Mlon:s last
wishes ylled the room.

ClaWton -eatherbourne distributed the legal docu,

ments sEelling out the e act amounts of inheritance. The
grouE comEared notes. 'll were smiling radiantlW as theW
left the conference room.

CHAPTER 23:

AH,

CALIFORNIA!

Winter in the Los Angeles basin is not at all

like winter in the northeast. There is no snow.

Toboganning and snow skiing might be happening high up in nearby mountains, but **El Lay** (as the Angelinos refer to it) headed to the beaches, outdoor sports, and balmy pastimes like golf, tennis, and shopping on Rodeo Drive. The main diIerence between summer and winter in **El Lay** is always in the taste of the air. xn summer it tastes oily with hints of soot and diesel. xn winter it is a pleasant mizture of oGone and dust. Any towns along the coast benePt from fresh onshore breeGes. Oo only two miles inland and the air layers invert and become a brown mizture of ezhaust fumes and industrial output. 2ollution is generally high. Rain is not in the picture for most of the winter months.

0n Thanksgiving Day MHMM it stormed. Rain poured

down. The 'c'urphy family gathered at 2hilip and
UeatherWs new sprawling estate on the coast in 'alibu.
Cmbrellas were parked outside the front door. Earmth
from the Preplace was welcomed. -onversation was
about the unusual weather and how pleasant it was to
have the air washed clean giving a break from eternal
summer.

The family had been home from their Buropean adF

venture for two months and had accomplished more
than any of them had believed possible. They had set up
a family nonFproPt charity organiGation. Kecause everyF
one donated millions, the organiGation was thriving and
giving away millions to many local nonFproPts including
the Lood Kank, the Lood Sitchen, the Y.A. Assistance
Yeague, 'others Against Drunk Drivers, the Koys and
Oirls -lub, -ANA, Uouse the Uomeless, Uabitat for UuF
manity, and Nunrise Uorse Uaven. xn these past two
months they had taken giant steps forward toward acF
tually helping those in need, even including some abanF
doned Appaloosas and 2alominos. An 0Jce had been
fully staled. 0utreach was jourishing.

Yegal papers incorporating a separate investigations

agency had been drawn up and Pled by the 2hilip 'cF
'urphy Yaw Lirm. The new corporation was dubbed
D"BRNW UA"DN. xt had begun looking into current and
past membership in the Klue Uand Nociety.

As the family, including Narah -. and qamboree q., sat
down for dinner lightning crackled on the horiGon. Kolts

1olted down into the distant ocean. The sky darkened.
The Prst rain in months continued to jood the streets.

2hilip raised a toast, 8Thank the Yord for a good rinsF
ing.!

Olasses clinked.

Then there was a loud strike at the front corner of the
house. The lights went out. Dishes rattled.

qamboree screamed.

Narah -. ducked under the table.

Seegan shouted, 8Olory Uallelu1ah.!

The rest of the party began to laugh. Yeave it Seegan.
Ue saw an adventure about to begin.

8At least the turkey is done. Bverything else is hot in

the oven. The bread wonWt be baked, but who cares,!
said Ueather. Nhe fetched candles, matches, and two
jashlights.

8x can sing for you,! suggested NarahF-.

A loud groan of 82YBANB "0! came from a dark corner
of the room. Narah sang an aria anyhow.

Dinner was candle lit and pleasant. The mashed

potatoes were cold, but the gravy was hot. The turkey was moist, but the ham was dried out. -ranberry sauce was heaped on. The green beans were undercooked, but the turkey stuJng was steaming. Then came spicey pumpkin pie with a mountain of whipped cream.

After dinner, 2hilip and Ueather, Saran and Ricardo,

and 'arielle with 2adrick ad1ourned to the library. All homes in this neighborhood had to have wood paneled libraries with ladders rolling around the room for high reach.

There were plenty of comfy chairs. Bveryone relazed with after dinner drinks.

8Ee do have a little problem to discuss,! said 2hilip.

8Ee have been home for two months and BlonWs body still has not been ezhumed.!

Ueather continued, 8"es, x am the coroner and x have

been intentionally delayed. "ou will recall that we disF cussed the ezhumation of BlonWs remains when we were on the -elebrity cruise a couple of months ago. Ee voted that we should have the body unearthed. x put in a re'uest while we were overseas. "othing happened. "o grave diggers. "o autopsy. "othing. x had made a mistake. x signed the death certiPcate, but x did not personally ezamine the body. Kecause this was the reF mains of a relative, x recused myself and asked a fellow ezaminer to take over. 0nce he had done his work, x simply signed oI. This is not unusual. Ee work in a huge county. There are ? HH deaths per week x cannot, or should x say, do not handle all of the re'uests for autopsies. Ee have a team of doctors who do the work. They are responsible for what we sadly call the NT02 A"D -U02. They video their work. They write out their Pndings. ThatWs where the train went oI the track. The doctor who was supposed to do a thorough autopsy was tanked.!

8The ezhumation did not happen, x launched an invesF

tigation into this doctorWs short comings. Cnfortunately, x found out more than x really wanted to know. The man is what they call a maintaining alcoholic.W Ue doesnWt drink on the lob. "o one could notice much wrong during work hours. Kut from the minute he got home until he passed out overnight, he was plowed. EeWre talking hammered, blasted, sloshed, and steamed. Uow do x know all of this Uis wife testiPed to it in court three days ago at their divorce proceedings.!

This guy Pled the report on Blon without even doing

the autopsy Ue blocked the paperwork for the ezhumaF tion because he knew he would be found out. Ue has been Pred. Eith cause. "ow x am trying to ezhume Blon without advertising that my own department has a serious problem.!

Ricardo took his leg oI the coIee table, decided not

the Pnish his drink, and said, 8Uoly crap Ee needed the autopsy information weeks ago. Eill it happen soon !

8Tomorrow, if the lights are on,! replied Ueather.

CHAPTER 24:

AUTOPSY

RESULTS

West Lawn Ceme tery was dry and warm as sum-

mer four days later when the cemetery crew and

backhoe operator could gnally bei.n the.r workE Mlon AcAurphy and h.s w.fe ,nielav hand been bur.ed .n s.de by s.de iraTesE Lhe cemetery workers were thankful for th.s because .t meant one iraTe to d.i upv one casketE

xast week they had been asked to eOhume a double

deepE 'ne huie oTerwe.iht casketE Lwo bod.es .ns.deE

'**She**6 had asked to be bur.ed on top of '**he**6 .n a loTer6s

embraceE Lh.s had been the.r 'usual pos.t.on throuihout

the.r 0I years of marr.aieE Lhe bur.al p.t was huieE Lhe

eOhumat.on and open.ni of loTers6 casket were irossE

Lhe husband d.d seem to haTe a sm.le on h.s faceE

,t Mlon6s bur.al s.tev the backhoe moTed .nE Sn m.nutes

Mlon6s iraTe was chewed open w.th the huie .ron scoopE

U.O feet of so.l were remoTedE , rope was attached to

the handles of the walnut coHn and t.ed to the hydraul.c
arm of the backhoeE Lhe hoe operator started to l.ftE
Lhe rema.n.ni d.rt fell oWE ,s the coHn drew eTen w.th
the iround the rope shredded and snappedE Lhe coHn
went crash.ni back down .nto .ts iraTe and broke open
w.th a deafen.ni soundE zncle Mlon6s body launched
out and ended up .n a s.tt.ni pos.t.on .n a sunl.t corner
of the iraTeE Lhe cemetery workers were creeped out
when they saw that h.s decay.ni face and hands were
lum.nescent blueE

 ,s d.Hcult and iross as .t wasv :eather d.d the au-

topsy herselfE Sn her m.nd she put on her autopsy hatE
'n her face she wore a look of d.spass.onate sc.ent.gc
eOplorat.onE B.th.n an hour she had eOam.ned all of
the .nternal oriansE Lhey were healthyv but they were
blueE :.s bra.n was remoTed and showed no s.ins of
,l(he.mer6sE :.s lunis were d.ssected and showed no
damaie from smok.ni or cancerE :.s k.dneys were cut
apart andv eOcept for typ.cal renal stonesv were perfectly
normalE Lhe autopsy came down to one d.sturb.ni factK
Glue sk.n and orian d.scolorat.on were present eTery-
whereE U.ck humor came to :eather6s m.nd when she
real.(ed that th.s was the grst truly blue-balled corpse
she had eTer seenE

Lwo days later the lab analys.s of Mlon6s body t.ssues

arr.Ted on :eather6s deskE Lhe results were degn.t.TeK
,riyr.a and acute hepat.c porphyr.aE Lhe former was
enT.ronmentalE Mlon had been po.soned dur.ni the last

month of h.s l.fe w.th collo.dal s.lTer result.ni .n acute

,riyr.aE Lhe only reason that no one saw the blu.ni of

h.s sk.n before he d.ed was h.s reclus.Te natureE :e l.Ted

aloneE :e must haTe been embarrassed to report h.s

unusual cond.t.onE Lhe latter was ienet.cK ,cute hepat.c

porphyr.a)P.ni Reorie6s d.sease" .s a blood d.sorder af-

fect.ni oOyien del.Tery to T.tal oriansE Lhe comb.nat.on

of collo.dal s.lTer and a ienet.c d.sorder had k.lled h.mE

 :eather contacted x.eutenant GeeGee Um.th6s oHce

to relay the gnd.nisE Lhe oHce secretaryv Cr.Tate ".chard

".ihton answeredE

 ?Yapta.n Um.th6s oHceEj

 ?Uhe6s been promotedNj asked :eatherE

 ? esv ma6amv last weekvj answered the pr.TateE

 ?Aay S speak to herNj asked :eatherE

 ?Aay S ask who .s call.niNj

 ?S6m :eather AcAurphyv the Younty YoronerEj

 ?S6ll put you throuih r.iht nowvj sa.d Cr.Tate ".ihtonE

 ?:ello Yapta.nE Yoniratulat.onsvj sa.d :eatherE

 ?S6m not sure S deserTe the promot.onE S was only do.ni

my ob oTer there .n Aess.navj sa.d GeeGeeE

 ? ot soE ou iuys took the bulletE Lhat k.nd of act.on

and braTery should be rewardedvj sa.d :eatherE

?Lhank youE S6ll adm.t that .f that6s what .t takes to be

promotedv S don6t need any more promot.onsE   owv how

can S help youEj

?S haTe results from Mlon6s autopsyE S bel.eTe he was

po.sonedE S need you to gnd out who d.d th.s and howvj
eOpla.ned :eatherE

 ?xet6s meetE Lh.s .s eOactly the break that we needE

Sf we gnd the murderer and l.nk h.m to the Glue :andv
we may be able to l.nk the xap.s Uoc.ety aiiress.on .n
Aess.na to the Glue :and .n SrelandE Be bel.eTe that
cr.m.nal drui peddl.ni .s the mot.Tat.onv but substant.Te
proof .s hard to come byE

CHAPTER 25:

A

CONNECTION

TO SICILY

The bullet wound from the gun bat tle in Messina

left Barbara Brandon Smith with a grazed scar on

her upper left forehead, an inch of skin and an inch of scalp. When she was getting ready to go to work in the mornings, she brushed her hair forward to cover the discoloration. She stared in the mirror and said aloud, "BASTARDS! You killed my friend Louis, wounded Sergeant Richardson, and Sergeant Lambert is still limping from your bullet to his leg. I am coming for you."

Since Messina she had tried to set up a full investigation into the Lapis Lazuli Society and its connections to the Blue Hand. Although she thought it would not be productive, she met with FBI agents. They said, "There is no indication of domestic harm to Americans. This is an oCshore problem, and it needs to stay oCshore."

She met with the Eentral Intelligence Agency. The lead

agent said, "Honey, this is America. That is Italy. We only investigate what is central to the intelligence of America. As far as we can tell, it is the Italians on Sicily who should straighten this out." He pronounced the word "Italians" as "qye-talians." When he called her "Honey," her trigger Onger had s'ueezed in tight two times.

Because her frustrations were growing, she contacted

Homeland Security and the Drug qnforcement Agency. She received similar responses. xne agent even told her, "Let them eat Biscotti. WeGll stick with Erispy Eremes." She was ve8ed. So she acted on her own within her

own department. She replaced Sergeant Larue with Her-cules Bosh whom she pried away from the L.A. Homicide Division by oCering promotion and the opportunity to in-vestigate international crimes. She also hired two rookie investigators. She wanted rookies because they would be thirsty to prove their worth.

The Orst stage of her investigation was to Ogure out

who had poisoned qlon McMurphy. She assigned Herc, her nickname for Hercules. Herc had no trouble Onding out that qlon McMurphy had contact with only two people. They were employees. xne was his housekeeper. The other was his mow-blow-and-go guy. The housekeeper was Angel 0uapa Eambionetto, a relative of Sarah E., qlonGs second wife. She was —j, decrepit in movement but shiny bright in personality:a little overweight but perfectly able to do her Pob if given the time. She still cleaned the house and would do so until the McMurphy relatives could decide what to do with the house and with her.

The other employee was Fabio Frankie 0iacometti, a

Ofty something Italian who spoke with an accent straight out of a Olm version of gangland Italy. qvery word had "eh" attached2 "Eigarette-eh," truck-eh, cat-eh, dog-eh." He had lived in America since he was Ofteen. His parents had immigrated from 3alermo. He had three brothers and three sisters, all devout Eatholics. There were N5 grandchildren.

Fabio still mowed qlonGs lawn, trimmed the bushes,

and pruned the trees. Because of FabioGs connection to Sicily, Herc suspected he had found the connection to the Eosa ?ostra 3alermo. 3alermo is the capitol of Sicily.3alermo per force would control the gang activity in Messina. Fabio needed to be followed.

Herc and the new hire, Sergeant Angela Marie 0ruen-

vold, began tailing Fabio. They tag teamed, one in an old beat up Ford pickup with a lawn mower and leaf blower loaded in back, one driving a ?issan Leaf.

xn Monday Fabio attended to three Hollywood es-

tates. He drove a brand new Ford FN'j pickup and all
of his lawn e'uipment was hauled behind in a new state
of the art four wheel 7atbed trailer. At the end of the Pob
at each property he met with an owner, at the Orst house
a man, at the ne8t the lady of the house, and at the last
another man. qach paid in cash and in each instance at
each property Fabio handed over a small brown paper
bag.

Herc and Sergeant Angela knew what was going on.

Late in the day Sergeant Angela met with Herc at the only BobGs Big Boy left in town.

xver burgers on outside tables, Angela said, "Whatever

happened to common senseK You knew this guy might be 4connected.G Why didnGt you bring a videographerK"

Herc pulled his i-phone out of his pocket and held it in

his palm while he handed it to her. He shook the phone as if to say, "Look what I have."

Angela 7ipped through the digital images. All of them

were dark or grainy. ?one of them were good enough to prove a drug deal had gone down.

Herc and Sergeant Angela followed Fabio again on

Tuesday. Fabio drove all of the way out to Malibu. The residence was a true ocean view mansion. Fabio spent the day cleaning, mowing, and trimming two fabulous coastal acres.

In late afternoon as the owner came down the stairs,

Angela drove up and asked Fabio for directions. Then she pulled two car lengths away and stopped seeming to search her navigation screen for the correct address.

xut of the home came the owner, the transaction took place. Angela pulled away in her silent car.

Herc and Sergeant Angela headed to a nearby coCee

shop. qspressos at midday would normally be too much caCeine. They ordered double shots anyway. This might prove to be a long day.

Angela Marie showed Herc the pictures. The wad of money was plainly visible. So were the faces of Fabio and the home owner. At Orst there was no evidence of drugs, but the home owner opened the brown paper lunch bag, reached in and pulled out a large baggie of white powder and two syringes. Both detective Herc and the sergeant knew that it was time to act. They had plenty of evidence to arrest Fabio. They could track him down and handcuC him.

Instead they drove to the L.A.3.D. owned store front

o ce that housed Eaptain SmithGs Oeld operations unit. Together with the Eaptain, Sergeant Lambert who was still limping, Sergeant Richardson whose arm was in a sling, and the other new recruit , Sergeant Billy 0on-salves, they planned the arrest of Fabio 0iocometti. It would happen later in the day if Fabio returned to qlon McMurphyGs garage as he usually did each day to sharpen tools and top oC his red plastic gallons of e8tra gas for his power tools.

At 25j p.m. all si8 of the police arrived at an empty

church parking lot three blocks from qlonGs property:no lights, no sirens, no identiOable markings on the cars. They walked to their target. FabioGs truck was in the driveway. The lights were on in the garage and in the house.

"Fabio must have a key to the house. Maybe heGs

helping himself to a beer," said Eaptain Smith.

"Angela and I will go to the front door. I want you other

four to spread out:two at the back door and two by the

garage. I will knock loud so that you know what is going

on."

Shortly after 25j she knocked. The front door dis-

integrated. Bullets from an automatic ri7e ripped into the porch railing and nearby trees. Eaptain BeeBee and Sergeant Angela had rocked back to the side Pust in time because of good tactical training.

Angela yelled, "Eome out with your hands up." Another

blast from the automatic tore the rest of the door oC its hinges.

The Eaptain crouched low, rolled across the threshold

and Ored twice. She hit her target. There was a loud crash as the body hit the 7oor. The household cat came running out in a streak and disappeared up the front tree.

Angela stepped inside holding the Eaptain back with

the motion of her palm backward and down. Then she screamed, "xH ?x!"

The housekeeper was dead on her back holding the

A she had been shooting. She had one bullet hole in the middle of her forehead and one in the middle of her AdamGs apple.

Fabio 7ed out the back door with a ?egro Modelo in his

Ost. He yelled, "DonGt shoot. IGm Pust here for the beer."

By noon the ne8t day the confrontation was sorted out.

Fabio was booked for drug peddling, but that was all. He had no weapons. He had nothing to do with the death of Mrs. Eombionetto.

xn the other hand, Mrs. EambionettoGs i-phone showed that, when the house was surrounded, she had te8ted a contact in 3alermo. The return te8t said, " ill them."

Eaptain Smith contacted I?TqR3xL ITALIA. It was only

then that she found out that the meek and innocent looking house keeper was the mother of the infamous Sicilian mobster, Alfonse Eapone. Interpol also revealed that her second son, Beneto Eapone, had been recently killed in a shootout in the town of Messina.

A search of qlonGs kitchen found two 'uarts of colloidal

silver and Ove one-gallon bottles of lemon 7avored ice tea, qlon McMurphyGs favorite drink. Finger prints were collected. A receipt was found. It revealed that the poison had been legally purchased in TiPuana one month before the death of qlon McMurphy.

CHAPTER 26:

MOVING

VANS

Karan and Ricardo

Karan and Ricardo no longer wanted to live in River-

side. Ricardo called it the Smog Capitol of Southern Cal-

ifornia. Ever since the National Campaign Against Dirty

Air in 2003 had found it to be one of the most polluted

regions in the United States, he had wanted to move.

They had looked at homes and sought jobs nearer the

coast for years. Jobs were available but homes at an a$ordable price were not. The closer a home was to the coast, the more it cost. And not just a small amount more. The home they had bought in Riverside in 2003 had cost 85P0,000. The same house within a mile or two of the ocean would have cost 82,P00,000. Brices had trended upward for years. Coastal homes were now worth a fortune.

Vut now, money was no object. They decided to move

to Balos Herdes and live in a home with a view out to
the ocean and across Redondo and Oermosa, the beach
towns. Ln a clear day they could see passenger jets
take o$ and land at X.A.W. Mith high powered binoculars
they could focus on Henice Veach and the far o$ cli$s
of :alibu. The location was perfect and on most days
the air was deliciousz clean, temperate, breathable. The
only problem was that, when the breeIe shifted and blew
o$shore, the manure pile from the horse property to the
west of them Klled their home with an odor that was
sickening. 'n "aranGs words it was pure shit and had
the taste of rotten eggs. The solution was easy enough
although it took three months. They Krst tried to ne-
gotiate odor abatement with their smelly neighbor. The
neighbor was insulted, refused, and o$ered an abrupt,
"xod damned liberals want to control everything.? Oe
pressed his :AxA hat farther down on his forehead. This
attitude persisted until "aran and Ricardo o$ered him
a choice he could not refusez two million more than his
property was worth. Then they tore down his house and
planted an eYtensive hillside garden. The air was once
again pure and the frustrations of life went away until
one evening they received a call from sister Oeather.

Oeather informed them that the family needed to

meet with the police, speciKcally Captain Varbara Vran-
don Smith and her team. "aran, who had answered the
call, swallowed hard and said, "Me just found our CAX:.
Now you want whatq?

Oeather wondered if "Knd your calm? was a new

Southern California eYpression like "xLLxXE TOAT SO'T? or "claiminG it.? She knew that Angelinos morphed English like wildKre burning in the Oollywood Oills. She respond-ed with, "7ou are not re1uired to be there. **But**, if youGd like to see justice for Uncle Elon and the people who were murdered in :essina, you ought to be there.?

"L.". weGll be there. 7our placeq? asked "aran.

"The meeting is set for day after tomorrow at Captain

SmithGs division head1uarters. 'Gll teYt you the address and time.?

Marielle, Padrick, and the Kids

:arielle and Badrick wanted the opposite of "aran and

Ricardo. They wanted to live in a nicer home than they had in Commerce with its industrial plants and rail yards. They did not want an elite, gated, suburban neighbor-hoods with private schools and privileged social norms. They decided that Tustin would be good. 't had well performing schools with a full racial miY. They wanted their children to grow up in what they thought would be a non-eYclusive sort of way. 't would be better if they had Spanish speaking friends. 't would be Kne to have

Vlack, Asian, and Hietnamese playfellows. :arielle was
concerned that the local school had bathrooms for VL7S,
x'RXS, and LTOER, but she swallowed her rigidity and
decided that it would all work out. She giggled to herself when she remembered reading a news article that
reported about a Southern California boy who identiKed

as a dog and wanted the right to go outside and pee on the lawn at school. Mhat was amaIing and hilarious was that his parents had gone to the school principal and eYplained that their child was "in his dog phase, and he has the right to pee where his dog identity tells him to pee.?

The new home was spacious. 't was built adjacent to

the last remaining Tustin strawberry Keld where strawberries that used to sell for Kfty cents per basket now sold for 89.2P. Tustin turned out to be a great place to live. The beach towns were reasonably close. Disneyland was only minutes away and cost only 869— for admission for a day. The air was breathable on most days with blue sky above and a brown layer of smog on the horiIon in the distance. The traFc was not bad unless you were caught in the rush hour between 3 p.m. and Zz30.

This almost ideal setting lasted for two months. Then

the sky fell in not Oenny Benny style but a slow rot of problems. The Krst distress happened when ten motorcyclists arrived on the familyGs front lawn. The leader, a rough and tumble bearded guy with blue and red twisting snake sleeve tattoos and hash tags below his eyes in light pink and pungent magenta, wore a T-shirt that advertised, "JESUS 'S OERE.? Oe eYplained that his club needed

86P,000 for their :LTLRC7CXES LR xLD :'N'STR7.

:arielle wondered if the leaderGs name was indeed Jesus,

but she did not ask. She eYplained that she represented

a family charity. The charity would welcome an online

grant application.

The leader shouted, "'tGs a NL? to his gang. They pealed out leaving ruts in the front lawn.

After that day, re1uests begging for money at the front

door and twice at the back patio were non-stop. Badrick hired a guard but that did not stop the money grubbers from arriving, being obnoYious, and demanding that the "rich need to give to the poor and needy.?

Then the SMATs started. Apparently some rejected

wingnut thought it would set the Rodrigueles straight if the police were informed that a major crime was hap-pening inside their home. The SMAT team arrived at 2 a.m., broke down the front door, handcu$ed Badrick, and scared the hell out of :arielle and the children. 't was daylight before the police Kgured out that this was a prank. This SMAT-ting happened twice more within the week.

That was the end of Badrick and :arielleGs stay in

Tustin. Mithin the month, they moved to Bhilip and OeatherGs :alibu community. 't was gated twelve feet up, and the guards carried holstered guns on their hips and ri es strapped around their shoulders. The only thing that was missing was xeneral Santa Anna style over shoulder bullet belts.

So it was that, when :arielle missed the call from her

brother, she did not bother to listen to his recorded message. 'nstead she walked two doors down and knocked on his door.

Bhilip and Oeather eYplained that they, meaning Ricar-

do, :arielle, Badrick, and "aran, would be meeting with Captain Smith tomorrow at — a.m. at the X.A.B.D. head-

1uarters. The police detectives needed help to complete the investigation into Elon :c:urphyGs death and to eY-plore the complicity between :rs. Cambionetto, Sicily, the Vlue Oand, and the bank account in urich.

CHAPTER 27:

THE

MEETING/THE

MONEY

The Los Angeles Police Departmen t was being

sued by CITIZENS WHO CARE (CWC), a local-vocal.

The CWC alliance wanted all things "police to be neutral in portrayal of their community." The lawsuit was an attempt to change the name of the Syndicates and Sociopaths unit. Syndicates and Sociopaths was, in the view of those doing the suing, "a negative representation of the citizens of our city." Funding was to be suspended until this "community predicament" could be sorted out.

"Good God, what do they want us to call these mobsters? Lilacs and Lilies?" said Sergeant Gruenvold.

"How about assholes and shitheads?" said Sergeant
Lois Richardson.

"Now girls, that's enough. We have visitors present,"
reminded Captain Smith.

"How about the Los Angeles Social Club?" contributed
Philip McCarthy.

Everyone laughed and relaxed.

Captain Smith started the serious part of the conver-

sation with, "I wanted everyone here today because we
have a serious problem. The L.A.P.D. will not fund further
investigation into what they call 'crimes committed outside the city.' The higher-ups say these crimes are for the
CIA or the FBI or Homeland Security and are nothing a
city police department should be involved in. Mind you, I
have checked with the CIA, the FBI, and Homeland. They
all refused to carry our case forward. I have only two
choices: 1) to stop the whole process, or 2) to ask you for
jnancial support."

"What support are we talking about?" asked Ricardo

putting his index jnger to his lips and peering at his often
too loud wife.

"Detective Bosh, Sergeant Gruenvold, and I would

need to Ky to Zurich and then to Sicily. We have information from a jle that the housekeeper, Angela Cambionetto, left behind. It should help us trace and close
down the Lapis Lazuli drug connection. It should help us
pin Elon's murder on them. The three of us would take
one week oY from our !obs. We would need money for

transportation, lodging, and food. We would have no way
to repay you. What do you think?"

 Jaran, who was bursting at the seams, blared, "UESV

WE ST WANT THIS B SINESS O ER AND DONE. WE
WANT STICE FOR O R BENEFACTOR, NCLE ELON."

 Heather uncovered her ears and said, "Believe it or

not, we have already talked this over. Each couple has set
aside one million dollars to make sure that the mystery
is solved and the criminals are prosecuted. Will that be
enough?"

 The Captain's !aw dropped open. Herc salivated. An-

gela smiled her pretty smile and gave a military salute to
the McMurphy's.

 The money was there. Now the investigation could
play forward.

CHAPTER 28:

THE ZURICH

BANK

The cross country non-stop ig ht on Unit ed Air-

lines landed at LaGuardia with a perfectly smooth

Air Force landing. The twelve mile transit on the I-678 freeway down to JFK International seemed fast. The Zight from JFK to burich International was an overnighter. As they landed the burich airport was hit jy a cross wind. The right wing of the ,et lifted high. The left wing almost nipped the ground. The landing was a slam-downN kavy styleN lize landing on an aircraft carrier. As if to empha-siCe the pointN the pilot jrazed hard and the passengers were thrown forward against their seat jelts.

 Saptain DmithN Betective MoshN and Dergeant Gruen-

vold znew they had arrived. Any ,et lag had jeen ,olt-ed out of them. They tooz the underground railway to the citiCen1H xotel on the river in the heart of burich downtown. They had chosen this hotel not only jecause

it would je safe and lu0uriousN jut also jecause it was
close to the Manz burich InternationalN the depository
janz that they were here to enter. This was the janz
that was indicated on the jlue parchment that they had
ojtained ,ust jefore the shoot-out in 1essina. My H$
a.m. they had checzed into the hotelN eaten jreazfast at
R7$ eachN and were ready to go.

 Their plan was simple.   They would walz the four

jloczs to the Manz burich down jy the Limmat EiverN
open the front doorN present their proof of account ac-
cessN and see where that would lead. The walz was jrisz
with a stiO jreeCe oO Laze burich that followed the out-
Zow of the river through downtown. Their arrival at the
janz was confusing. There was no entrance on the street
side unlize all of the other jusinesses stepping their
advertising and professionally arranged window displays
out front with doors opening onto the sidewalzs. Instead
they were confronted with no door at all and a rela-
tively small metal and glass impenetrajle fortress. kear
the rooZine were small numjers and letters identifying
MAkK bUEISx IkT5EkATIWkAL 3767 Manholfstrasse. The
threesome znew they were at the correct addressN so
they continued around the juilding on a steepN well gar-
dened pathway to the riverfront. At that point they saw

stairs that would surely lead them to the entrance to the janz. Up they went. qhen they reached the topN they were ajout "$ feet from three granite steps leading to a massive glass door.

They stepped forward and were immediately jlasted jy an ear splitting high pitched s?ueal. They ,umped jacz and heard a jass voice grumjleN "This is MUILBIkG 3767. qhat jusiness have you hereYP

The L.A. police were amaCed. xow did this juilding

znow to speaz 5nglish and not the Alemannic Dwiss German of the cityY They were not sure what to do.

Saptain Dmith shoutedN "qe come in peace. qe have

a priority admissions code that we were given jy 1rs. Angela Samjionetto.P Dhe did not try to e0plain that Angela Samjionetto was dead and that they found the admissions code woven into the hem of her jlacz Dunday dressN the one with Eosary jeads on the hangar and a devotional in the poczet.

The juilding saidN "9ou do not need to shoutN Saptain Dmith. 2lease hold the code card high up.P

Saptain Dmith reached into her purseN pulled out the

code cardN and held it high. Dhe wondered how in hell this juilding had 4gured out her name and ranz.

Duspecting that their ear drums might je jlast-

ed againN the threesome stepped forward as the door opened. Wnce inside they found that everything was computeriCed. ko people.

The MUILBIkG spozeN "Insert the admission card into the slot.P

That was easy. There was jut one slot lit in red in an

otherwise jlanzN shiny metal wall. In went the card and up went the wall revealing elevator doors.

"2lease proceedNP spoze MUILBIkG 3767.

They did so and in seconds were electronically led to a small room with comfortajle chairs. A panel in the wall

opened and a shelf slid out. Wn the shelf were a janz
deposit jo0 and a leather jound ledger.

Three hours later the team had found incriminating

evidence. FirstN there was a handwritten list of the memjers of the Irish Mlue xand Dociety. ke0t came a list
of the memjers of the Dicilian Lapis LaCuli Dociety. A
lengthy ledger account of deposits was ne0t. Beposits
to the Mlue xand Dociety started in H8:8. They came
from janzs in Shicago and kew 9orz Sity. The jalance
was 'N''7N"66N8'7 highly stajle Dwiss francs that would
convert to 'Nà8àN':HN::H American dollars. Beposits to
the Dicilian Lapis LaCuli came to twenty times that muchN
nearly 3$ jillion dollars.

 qithdrawals from the Mlue xand Dociety totaled over

two jillion dollars across the yearsN all of it going to char-
itajle organiCations. qithdrawals from the Dicilian Lapis
LaCuli Dociety were RH3 jillionN all of it going to individuals
whose names and addresses on Dicily were listed in large
jlue type. 1ost of these addresses were in 2alermo and
second most were in 1essina.

 A stunning fact was found. Beposits from the Dicilian

jranch jegan in H:8HN nothing jefore that. The 4rst deposit was eight jillion dollars and it came from the owner of a well znown American pharmaceutical company'
2urtoo 2harma. This inZow of cash from America would
need to je carefully traced. 2erhaps a jigger criminal
4sh was in the net.

 Wnly a few small pieces of information at the jacz

of the ledger might help prove who was responsijle for
the death of 5lon 1c1urphy. First was 5lonVs name with

the words "deve essere eliminato.P' DecondN large print
statedN "Lo far/ Franconi Samjionetto.P"

The Los Angeles s?uad wrote down names and num-

jers. They placed the deposit jo0 and ledger jacz on
the e0tended shelf. qhen they stood upN the shelf disappeared into the wall. They joarded the elevator and
at the jottom they tried to e0it the janz.

The MUILBIkG spozeN "ko papers may go with you.P
xercules wadded up the notes he had written and

threw them on the Zoor. xe was not worried jecause he
had used his phone to record the contents of the entire
ledger.

The MUILBIkG saidN "9ou made a mess. 2lease leave.
Auf qiedersehen.P

Saptain Dmith needed to taze care of one impor-

tant transaction jefore leaving the juilding. Dhe saidN
"MUILBIkG 3767N I choose to close the account we ac-
cessed while we were upstairs.P

"I call itN)U2 5L5#ATWENV not upstairs. Bo you have the
Kill SodeYP aszed the MUILBIkG.

Saptain Dmith paniczed. "Kill SodeYP she aszed.

"It is the K.S. on your admissions code cardNP said 3767.

"qould that je KS''IkT5E2WL!ITALIA!2EIWEIT9 'MYP aszed the Saptain.

"9esN it would je. kow you must choose one of the followingNP said 3767.

Hó. Slose this account and transfer all funds to interpol account 37b

'ó. Slose Mlue xand Account

"ó. Slose Lapis LaCuli Account

àó. Transfer Mlue xand Funds

3ó. Transfer Lapis LaCuli Funds

6ó. Duspend all transactions for H month

7ó. Duspend all transactions for 6 months

8ó. Duspend all transactions permanently

"xoly crap P whispered Saptain Dmith.

"xoly crap is not an appropriate choiceNP said the

MUILBIkG.

The conversation jetween Dmith and 3767 continued

in a lengthy and diCCying e0change. Saptain Dmith transferred all Lapis funds over to the Mlue xand Dociety. Then
she impounded the Mlue xand account transferring the
huge jalance to an Interpol holding account.

Dhe thanzed the MUILBIkG even though she was not

sure who or what she was thanzing. All three Salifornians
were glad to e0it into the normal world.

In minutesN Marjara MrandonN xerculesN and Angela

1arie were jacz at their hotel ensconced in plush seats
at a tajle near the jar. MeeMee ordered a doujle TitoVs.
xercules wanted a 1anhattan with a shot of AjsintheN

and Angela ordered a pitcher of 2atr n margaritas and
salt rimmed glasses. They smiled at each otherN laughedN
and decided that they would taze a day oO and visit the
city sites all of the ne0t day.

Later in the day Saptain Dmith called 2hilip 1c1urphy

zeeping the ten hour time diOerence in mind. It was
mid-morning in L.A. ko one answered. 2hilip was at

worz. The Saptain left a message saying that her team had made tremendous progressN that they were way under judgetN and that she would call again in a few days. Dhe did not spell out any of the janz ledger details for fear that the phone call might je traced.

H The name of this hotel is spelled with a small "c.P

citiCen1. 2erhaps this means any common citiCen will je admitted. The price says otherwise.

' "xe needs to je eliminated.P
" "Franconi Samjionetto will do it.P

CHAPTER 29:

RETURN TO

SICILY

From Zurich the Los Angeles team took the train

to Rome. Captain B.B. Smith had arranged to meet

Capitano Giovanni Bertolini at a division of Al Italia Interpol in the Monti district near the Coliseum. Capitano
Bertolini headed the Indagini Malativa De Sicilana.1

On the train from Zurich to Rome, Captain Smith,

Detective Bosh, and Sergeant Gruenvold had thought through the diwculties and dangers of entering Messina again, alone and bithout kacTup. yheir last visit had ended in disaster. yhe possikilitN of another gun kattle bas high. SurelN the Cosa Lostra zapis zaJuli bould Tnob that their kanT account bas dissolved. BN nob the island maVa bould Tnob that Captain Smith had shot and Tilled Angela Camkionetto, the matriarch of the Capone line and godmother to Poseph 2alachi, the most violent

of them all. She had also keen involved in the Tilling of
Beneto Capone at the gunVght in Messina last Near.

 jerhaps it bas not bise to return to SicilN.   jer-

haps sleeping dogs should continue to sleep. I cani che
dornono non mordono.E On the other hand, the z.A.
threesome Tneb that revenge bas the batchbord of the
Cosa Lostra. Revenge could reach across continents.
yheN bere no safer in Southern California than theN
bould ke in Messina or anN other Sicilian tobn. yheN
needed to purge the zapis zaJuli memkers. yheN banted
to arrest, deport and prosecute Alphonse Capone. yheN
sought qustice for 'lon McMurphN and his Tin.

 yhe z.A. sxuad decided that theN bould seeT help

from SicilN"s neb Chief of jolice, Capitano Bertolini. AnN
approach to the Sicilian mok had to ke carefullN planned
and eòecuted, or it bas not to ke attempted at all.

 Because Capitano Bertolini bas in charge of Messina
mok investigations, he formed a plan xuicTlN.

 àCi3 richieder0 un platone di trenta. In inglese Nou saN,

be need "W, a platoon, bell-armed, readN to arrest or
Till manN uomini cattivi," the borst ones.Y yhe Capitano

tbirled the ends of his handlekar moustache ketbeen his
thumks and foreVngers.

àHe, uh, no, I go to Messina joliJia Stradale all"iniJio.

I mean be go Vrst to police. He get help. He surround
and close dobn the neb zapis zaJuli Sede centrale. ?ou
saN headxuartererJ. He must invogliare. Fob Nou saN it4
'ntice Signor Capone so he bill ke there. 5irst be give
him some information that his enemN, Capitana Smith
bill ke there. yhen he bill ke there.Y

Hhen all "$ police, including Capitano Bertolini and his

platoon and the three from California, sped through the
Messina harkor in a police patrol koat, all bas xuiet. It
bas middaN. jeople on the streets sab them and ducTed
into shops, kars, and anN availakle open door. yhe scene
reminded Fercules of an American Hild Hest movie.
Clint 'astbood enters Deadbood bith his righteous men.
yhe streets clear.

Capitano Bertolini led the baN to the baterfront police

department. A neb man, zieutenant Montkleu, bas nob
in charge of the StaJione di joliJia at the harkor. 'nlisting
his help bas easN. Fe agreed to help àclean up his tobn.Y
Fe o9ered 1è fullN armed troupers to àensure success.Y
And he agreed that a !6è,WWW incentive paNakle to his
favorite charitN bould guarantee that Alphonse Capone
bould ke at the zapis zaJuli headxuarters bhen theN
surrounded it.

yhe afternoon bent xuiet as the police approached

the target on the Street of Blood. yhe headxuarters
occupied an ancient Catholic church, Mother MarN of the
Innocents. yhe font out front bas Vlled bith holN bater.
yhe sign attached to it said in koth Italian and 'nglish,
àDip Nour right hand in and then bet Nour forehead bith

the sign of the cross.Y ybo passing priests did so and disappeared inside the FolN Door. As theN bent in, three alleN cats scurried out chasing a rat.

 Capitano Bertolini used a kullhorn to address the

church.àLon teniano a te nessum danno. O9riamo una soluJione per la tua vendetta. yi forniremo giustiJia.Y$

 yhe Capitano bas readN for the ansber. So bere Bee-

Bee, Fercules, and Angela. As the stained glass rose bin-
dob akove the FolN Door eòploded in glittering shards,
theN hit the ground and rolled up kehind fountains and
statuarN. Captain Smith turned to maTe sure that the
local trouper team bas still in place so that the signal to
advance and overtaTe the church might ke given. Hhat
she sab turned her stomach. yhe Messina police sxuad
bas running abaN carrNing their kullet proof shields kehind their kacTs for protection. She xuicTlN realiJed that
she could not klame them. yheN lived here. yheN had
families.

5rom bithin the church a loud speaTer sNstem announced, àDonna Smith U una putana. zei morir0 Yè
M-"W machine gun Vre from inside the church kleb

through the FolN Door. Grenades bere throbn out into
the plaJa. Shrapnel sliced through Sergeant Angela"s
thigh. She screamed kut managed to lok a ash grenade
through the klobn out FolN Door. RjGs bere launched
into the church from the sides, the front, and the kacT.
yhe klasts bere deafening. FistorN repeated itself. yhe
roof over the nave collapsed. yhe kell tober fell into the
transept, and the mightN front markle pulpit collapsed

forbard across the altar and front pebs. yhe Fouse
of God bas decimated. yhe onlN thing unscathed bas a
markle statue of MarN and kakN Pesus protected in an
alcove shrine.

BN middaN much of the rukkle had keen cleared. 5if-

teen kodies bere kagged including tbo priests. Sounds
could ke heard coming from the ossuarN crNpt keneath

the altar platform of the church. A kacThoe bas driven through the rukkle. yhe crNpt granite over-stone mono-lith bas lifted. Belob bere Alphonse Capone and Vve of his capos. All of them bere semi-conscious, bounded, and kroTen. Alphonse had lost an eNe, one ear, and his right arm from mid humerus on dobn. 'mergencN action Tept him from kleeding out. Fis eNekall bas picTed up o9 the oor and iced. Fis ear bas nobhere to ke found. Fis trigger Vnger bas hanging from his hand kN a thin strip of kloodN sTin.

Angela Gruenvold had passed out. Captain Smith se-

cured a tournixuet to her leg and bent to looT for Fer-cules. Fe bas picTing glass from his left hand and his scalp. She then searched the vestikule. She found a dam-aged old desT bith a neb laptop inside. She hid the com-puter in the kodice of her klouse keneath her kulletproof vest. She told no one. yhe daN ended as it had kegun. Lo kirds sang. Lo cars hummed. Lo merchants habTed. Silence. Lothing kut silence and dust in the air.

1 Investigations of Sicilian nderborld

E Sleeping dogs do not kite.

" Bad men.

$ He mean Nou no harm. He o9er a solution for Nour

revenge. He bill provide Nou bith qustice.

è yhe Smith boman is a kitch. She bill die.

RocTet jropelled Grenades

CHAPTER 30:

TRUE

INHERITANCE

Months ewb y.P i hlpla dnH rwdth wT were busy

with their jobs and taxiing the boys to school,

sports events, and piano and violin lessons. Declan was

reading up about college entrance. He wanted to be-

come a lawyer just like his dad. He decided that he would

become the legal representative for the new McMurphy Family Foundation. He wanted to invite Bill Gates to be a board member. Together they would tackle homelessness in Los Angeles.

Keegan wanted to be a race car driver. He saw himself speeding through Monaco, winning the race, and giving the winnings to crippled and injured drivers who had never crossed the :nish line.

The McMurphy Family Foundation had grown. There was money to advertise and market whatever the Foundation wanted to accomplish. The goals were lofty. The Foundation established :ve main divisionsS

Division to Reek Rolutions for Homelessness
Uesettlement Division for Afghan and Ckrainian Uefugees

Vancer Uesearch Funding Division
Dogs for Eeterans
An 'ndowment for the Rociety for the Blind
The McMurphyPs, including Ohilip, Heather, Karan, Ui-

cardo, Marielle and Oadrick, all were board members. They wrote a charter that would ful:ll Cncle 'lonPs last wishes. They dedicated themselves to helping oth-ers. If course, that was tricky business because giv-ing away money was treacherous at times. Avoiding greedy, self-serving wheeler dealers meant extensive re-search, background checks, and a long list of internet and gumshoe investigations in order to avoid being swindled. 6t was one thing to be humanitarian. 6t was entirely another to be philanthropically stupid.

 Karan and Uicardo attended all board meetings with-

out fail. The meetings had been much more comfortable since Uicardo had signed Karan up with a speech thera-

pist. The therapist, a pleasant 7 foot 3 inch ex-basket-
ball star :rst took Karan to an empty gym and recorded
KaranPs normal speaking voice. 6t echoed. 6t boomed.
6t was loud like a wrecking ball on a steel building. That
recording was then compared to recordings of a freeway,
a train at midnight, unfed babies in a nursery, and similar
sounds with high decibels. Top of the list was the 0zz

ton Great Bell of Dhamma/edi in BurmaWnow Myanmar. Karan was embarrassed to have to admit that her voice had the tone of a 0zz ton bell. Maybe she needed a new clapper. Rhe got the point. Jith her new therapist she began practicing speaking in what she thought to be a whisper.

Marielle and Oadrick were over-busy with their chil-

dren. There were dance lessons swimming lessons, horseback riding competitions, piano, golf, and singing. The children had no time for i-Ohone or i-Oad. They were abnormal. They were outside. They were playing with friends. They were happy. Marielle and Oadrick ended each day exhausted but smiling.

qamboree q. and Rarah V. moved in together. They

did not dislike each other as much as they imagined. Jhen a penthouse condominium became available in the Hollywood Towers, they set aside their di l erences. 'ight thousand s)uare feet on the :fteenth Noor gave them enough room so that they could live alone when they needed to. They signed a pact with three strict intentionsS

2X. Zo men because they are pigs.

4X. Zo men because they pee on the bathroom Noor.

0X Zo men because there is a Norist in the lobby who

can deliver Nowers every day of the week.

 Vlayton Jeatherbourne gave up on the gay scene.

His one-time romance with "avier "enon had ended in

shallow, self-serving disappointment. He moved to the Bahamas after his divorce and married a bikini, 00 years old, blonde and thin, and able to make a mean margarita. He never did remember her last name. His wife, eeee, married a ten year younger man. He worshipped the ground she walked on. To make sure that the ground that she walked on stayed sacred, eeee bought a private island in the Maldives and learned to scuba dive, to sail, and to :sh for marlin.

In the :rst of qune 4z48, the McMurphy group met

with Vaptain Rmith, Detective Bosh, and Rergeant Gruenvold in the luxurious third Noor conference room of Ohilip and HeatherPs villa. The view of the Oaci:c was stunning.

6t had taken months for the police group to fully in-

vestigate the criminal activities of the Lapis La/uli Rociety. Zow it was time to report their results.

9Vaptain Rmith, we are anxious to hear what you

have found out. But :rst, we did receive your account of the expenses for your investigation. They come to "432, 233.zz. My brothers and sisters and 6 have talked it over and we want to give you the residual balance . Je originally set aside three million for you. After expenses, that leaves "4,34Y,Y40 in the bank. Divided by three that is "ézé,7zY for each of you. Je will pay all tax conse)uences for you,' said Ohilip.

9Rtate law will not allow us to receive extra pay for our work,' said Vaptain Rmith.

9Zo problem. This is not extra or enhanced pay. 6t is a gift from us to you. Because it is far above the maximum

.

that Valifornia allows for gifts, we are also paying a tax penalty. But that is what we have unanimously decided to do for you because of the peace of mind you have given us. 5ou risked your lives. 5ou went far above what we expected. LetPs call this a little gratitude for a lot of accomplishment,' said Ohilip as he stood up, :lled wine glasses with Orosecco, gave a stem to everyone, and proposed a toast.

9HerePs to a job well done.'

BeeBee, Hercules, and Angela were stunned. They

stood up and clinked glasses all around. After everyone settled back into their seats, Vaptain Rmith spoke.

9There really isnPt any way to thank you enough. 5our

generosity is something unheard of. 6 do think that you will enjoy hearing about almost all of what we have done. LetPs approach this with an old clich S **ErG ODD,B ErG AN,B NU, ErG LOYW**. The **ODD,** is that we closed down the Lapis La/uli account in Rwit/erland. The residual balance was over 8z billion dollars, all of it tied to drug peddlers and pushers. The con:scated money is about to be transferred to your McMurphy Family Foundation with the explicit re)uirement that it is to be used to create drug rehabilitation facilities in Vhicago, Zew 5ork, and Messina, 6taly.'

Vaptain Rmith was shaking her head 95'R' and so were

the rest of the people in the room. Rhe handed the Noor over to Detective Bosh.

He said, 96 guess we should call this next bit the **AN,**

UGS . Zo gang member in Ricily will be prosecuted. The authorities on the island say that all of the guilty were

killed when the roof of Mother Mary of the 6nnocents
collapsed. 6 believe you already know that Alphonse
Vapone, son of the housekeeper and matriarch Angela
Marie Vambionetto, died of his wounds three weeks after
we departed the island. Repsis rotted in his eye socket
and inside the canal of his missing ear. He died in insane
agony screaming, 6 will kill them all. 6n my lifetime they
will be dead. Those American whores and Americans
who suck donkey dicks.P Olease forgive me for even saying
that much.'

Blushing slightly, he continued, 9The **AN, UGS** is not

all bad. Vapitano Bertolini, chief of Ricilian Oolice, has received new funding for extra troupers and ammunition.
Oerhaps he will be able to make a dilerence. Zow for
the **LOYW**. Rergeant Gruenvold, will you please do the
honors.'

  Angela Gruenvold limped to the window, slid it

open a few inches, and inhaled the fresh ocean bree/e.
Rhe turned and faced her benefactors whom she now
thought of as friends.

  9The **LOYW** could not be uglier. The bulk of the forty

billion dollars in the bank in $urich came from prof-
its from the illegal sale of oxymorphonecodone. Rtreet
name oxy-M. This drug was created, manufactured, and
distributed by the Henry Rtackler drug labs, the labs we
all know by their tabloid name, Oertoo Oharmacological.
Oertoo created the drug for elective pain relief. Oertoo
knew that its oxymorphonecodone was highly addictive
across all ages and races, but they buried that information. 6nstead, Oertoo blit/ed doctors, pharmacies and

the general public with advertisements proclaiming the
safety and e cacy of their product. As it turns out,
all lies. A true case of evil begets evil. And the ugly
news is that not one single Rtackler family member will
be prosecuted. 6nstead they will pay a nominal :ne of
around eight billion dollars and will shut down Oertoo
Oharmacological. An eight billion dollar :ne is nothing
to Henry Rtackler because it is estimated that he still
has z billion in pro:ts invested in bramble of holdings
throughout the Cnited Rtates, Vanada, and 'urope. 6 do
not want to be cartoonish and say, THATPR ALL FILKR,P
but that really is astonishingly all. The rich got richer. The
crimes of the elder Rtacklers most certainly will not be
visited upon the younger Rtacklers.'

 An awkward silence followed for a few minutes. Then

Heather declared, 9All is well. Cncle 'lonPs wish is being
ful:lled. Je are doing what he could not do. Je are
trying to help people who genuinely need help. May we
continue to do good in this world. Iur true inheritance is
to give away as much of 'lonPs money as we can.'

Author JebsiteS charleshansonbooks.godaddy.com

Made in the USA
Las Vegas, NV
04 January 2024

83874675R10173